WHO TOOK JESUS OUT OF CHRISTMAS?

A Marlee Madison Mystery

Sharon Brunnelson

ISBN 978-1-0980-0543-6 (paperback)
ISBN 978-1-0980-0544-3 (digital)

Christian Faith Publishing, Inc.
832 Park Avenue
Meadville, PA 16335
www.christianfaithpublishing.com

Printed in the United States of America

To Blake + Brice
   Enjoy and celebrate
Christmas every day!

11/9/19

To my wonderful husband and all my family: you are my great-
est blessing in life. God is good, and I thank him every day for each
one of you.
   And to everyone who loves the Lord!

Sharon Brunnelson

Prologue: 1873

Jedediah Christmas Smith returned to his cabin cold, wet, and tired. He put another log on the fire and stoked it back to life so he could heat his coffee and dry his saturated clothing. His mission had taken longer than expected. The deed was finished. He was glad it was over and done with.

Smith was tired of the gold. He had found a lot of it, more than he could spend in many lifetimes. But the gold had proved to be a curse as much as it was a blessing.

On the positive side, he had built a church, a parsonage for the pastor, a town hall, a schoolhouse, and a dry goods store. He had been able to secure a doctor for the town and, of late, a sheriff. The gold had allowed him to help his best friend, Hiram Trumbull, to build both a house and the Inn.

On the negative side though, it brought a lot of troublesome and unseemly men who came to town with all manner of schemes, both to find gold themselves or to cheat those who had out of theirs. They had built the saloon, and lately, there had been a lot of trouble in town, all stemming from that establishment. There were a lot of con artists who had arrived, and he had stopped counting how many long, lost brothers he had.

He had to hire a couple of lawyers who were kept busy checking their stories. None had ever proved to be true. Smith was orphaned on the day of his birth, Christmas Day, 1829, so he gave up thinking he would ever discover who his mother was, or if he did have any real family.

Along with being bothered by a host of fictitious brothers, he had also been physically threatened. Some had even tried to black-mail him, but Smith only laughed at these efforts. "You can't black-mail a man who has had all his sins forgiven by Jesus," he told them.

He sipped his coffee and was glad for its heat and the heat of the fire. For now, the gold was hidden, and it could stay that way. He didn't care if it ever got found. So, let them come look for it, it wasn't his responsibility any longer.

It seemed God was protecting the gold for some reason. There were hundreds of treasure hunters who had come to town, but most of them remained empty-handed. No one found out where Smith had discovered his.

"Well, Lord, you give, and you take. I'll leave it up to you to decide who should find the gold and when. I have all I need for the rest of my life, for which I am grateful."

Jedediah Smith refused to live in town. Not only did he prefer the beauty of this mountain, he felt it brought him closer to the Lord living up here. Smith was glad to be away from the trouble that followed him when he went down the mountain.

He looked forward to the day when all the treasure hunters would finally give up and move on. Since they never found much gold, he thought it would just be a matter of time, and then the town would be at peace. He prayed for the treasure hunters that they would turn to Jesus, but that prayer wasn't often answered.

Maybe the townspeople could force the saloon out of business one day. Not much good came from that place. He hoped someday the town would be able to turn it into a better establishment.

It would be Christmas soon. The town was preparing for their annual Christmas celebration he started five years ago. It was the least he could do to honor the *one* who saved his soul. It drew the town together and pointed them to the real purpose for the holiday season.

He was warm enough now to turn in. Tomorrow, he would go back down the mountain. He promised Hiram he would come to help him since Hiram was putting some finishing touches on his house.

"Thank you, Lord, for the blessing of my friend." God sent him Hiram, and he was more than a brother. Hiram and his wife saved his life when he had been caught in a snowstorm that first year. He had offered Hiram part of the gold, but he turned it down flat. *Not too many human beings were made that way,* Smith thought.

"Lord, I have a wonderful life because of you. I'll do all I can to honor you in this town and tell everyone why you came."

That's why he named the town Christmas. He hoped and prayed the town would have a legacy to live on after he was gone. That didn't look too promising right now, and he wasn't even sure the town would be here fifty years from now. Too many towns died when the gold rush ended.

"Well, Lord, the town and the gold belong to you. I sure hope you have something special planned for the people who come to live here. You sure blessed me with that gold. So, I'll leave it up to you if you want someone else to have it."

CHAPTER I

Marlee: 2018

Marlee Madison was not quite sure she wanted to turn thirteen. Her given name was Martha Lee, but no one called her that except her grandmother. The name, Martha, came from her mother's ancestor, Martha Washington. And because her mother was also a descendant of the famous Lee family of Virginia, all the women in her family received the middle name, Lee. No one in town knew that Marlee was not her given name, and she was more than happy to keep it that way.

Marlee was more of a tomboy than a princess. She was happier to explore the wooded hills above her hometown of Christmas than to lock herself in her room to paint her nails or style her hair.

She could outpace her best friend, Jeremy Jordan, Jem for short, in running, hiking, and climbing trees, oh, and in digging worms for fishing, a skill no other girl in her middle school class came close to matching, nor wanted to.

Her unruly red hair was her mother's undoing as Marlee seldom brushed it out, so it took nearly an hour of detangling to get it braided. Keeping Marlee still for any length of time was a significant undertaking.

Marlee sighed as she stared at her reflection in the mirror and took stock of her once again tangled hair, sunburned face, thin frame, broken nails, and skinned knees. She wondered if becoming a teenager meant she would have to, as her grandmother put it, "become a young lady." Marlee wasn't sure what that phrase even meant.

I hope it doesn't mean I have to stop climbing trees, she thought to herself. After all, climbing trees was a most useful skill if you were lost in the woods or needed to get away from a bear quickly. Though in all of her years exploring, Marlee had only seen bears from way off and had never surprised one up close.

Does it mean I can't fish anymore? she wondered. But surely there were female fishermen, or did they call them fisherwomen?

Dad blast it, I don't want to be a young lady. I like the way I am now, she said to herself. But Marlee knew she had no choice because tomorrow was coming, and she would have to give in to being thirteen and accept the changes that were coming.

Birthdays at the Madison household were as special as Mom could make them for Marlee and her brother, Parker, on the family's limited budget. Mom always made their favorite dishes, and Marlee knew she would get homemade gifts as folks in Christmas usually just "got by." Still, Marlee was thankful there were plenty of townsfolk to pitch in when times were tough because times were almost always tough for the residents of Christmas.

Marlee figured she would get a new sweater since her mother loved to crochet and was an expert at it. She hoped she'd also get a couple of new ChapSticks. Marlee loved the special flavored ones. Her mom told her she could start wearing a little lip color when she turned thirteen, but Marlee was just as happy to keep using her ChapStick.

She loved the ones flavored chocolate, but those were hard to come by. You could only get them at Christmastime and only by driving into Henderson where they had a Walmart and a Target. Henderson was the closest big city to Christmas and was about forty miles away. It was big enough to have several shopping malls, a multiplex theater with big screens, a hospital, plenty of restaurants, and best of all, a library where you could use the Internet. Christmas didn't have any Internet, and there wasn't any cellphone service either, so not too many people had cellphones, just the adults and only if they needed them for their jobs.

Christmas still looked the same as it did in the1940s and didn't even have a McDonalds, although you couldn't beat Belle's and Beaus for food whether you wanted it fast or not. Most folks didn't mind waiting for it, and Belle nearly never had anyone ask for carryout as everyone in this area stayed to visit over their meals.

The town had a small theater, but it didn't show any current movies, only ones available long after the DVDs were released. It was only open on Fridays and Saturdays, and once in a while a holiday if Mr. Maxwell thought he could drum up enough customers to make it worth his while to come in. There was also Caldwell's Hardware and Mercantile, which everyone called the H & M. That was where most of the townsfolk got their necessities. There were some smaller businesses like a barbershop, a beauty shop, and a dry cleaner. Then, of course, there was Dr. Millman's clinic where everyone went when they needed a doctor.

Parker was three years older than Marlee. His best friend, Liam, had worked all summer at the H & M. Marlee's mom had been on Park to find a summer job, but he mostly dillydallied about it. Now it was almost school time, and Park had only managed to do a couple of yards around town each week. Still, Mom said it was always a help with the extra bills they were causing her because they were growing up.

Liam's younger brother, Patrick, was Marlee's age and hung around her and Jem once in a while, but he wasn't much for out-door stuff. Patrick was one of those strange kids who liked it better indoors where he could read and study math and science. He was the school brain and even won the county science fair not once, but twice. Everyone thought Patrick was the smartest kid in the county and figured he'd someday take over for Dr. Millman.

Marlee's thoughts were interrupted by her mother calling her to supper. *My last supper*, she thought. She was sure she would never eat again once she reached this dreaded milestone.

"I'm coming, Mom," she yelled down. Marlee rushed into the bathroom to wash up and make herself as presentable as possible.

She ran downstairs and just as she pulled her chair out from the dining room table, her mother said, "Hold on, young lady, I need you to help me get the food on the table."

"Where's Park? Why can't he help?" Marlee mumbled. Fortunately, her mother was back in the kitchen and didn't hear her or she knew she'd be given extra chores for complaining about this one.

By the time they all sat down, Marlee was quite hungry. She figured this wouldn't be her last supper after all, as her mother did wonders with food. How you could make vegetables taste good enough to eat them was a miracle only her mother and Miss Belle could work.

"Your father promised he'll be home in time for your birthday tomorrow, Marlee," her mother said. Jenna Lee Madison was almost as excited as her daughter that her husband had promised to arrive in time for Marlee's birthday.

"That's good, Mom. I wish I didn't have to turn thirteen. But having Dad home will make it more tolerable, I guess." Marlee hung her head down and looked at her plate.

"I never heard of a young girl not wanting to become a teenager," her mother said, surprised that Marlee was not looking forward to her birthday.

"Yeah, being a teenager ain't any different than being a kid, just older," her brother interjected.

"Isn't," their mother corrected him.

"Ain't or isn't, there's no difference in turning thirteen," he said and shrugged.

"That's because you're a boy. If you were a girl, you wouldn't say that." Marlee was sure every girl would agree with her.

"All right, children. Parker, please say grace."

As they all bowed their heads, their dog, Sox, started barking wildly as the front door opened.

"Am I late for supper?"

"Daddy!" "Dad!" "Trent!" everyone said in unison. They all pushed back their chairs and ran to the hallway where Trent Madison was setting down his bag and hanging up his jacket. He opened his arms for hugs from everyone.

"I thought you weren't coming home until tomorrow!" Mrs. Madison exclaimed.

"Feed me, and I'll explain everything. I'm famished. I didn't stop for anything since breakfast," Mr. Madison said as he took his usual place at the table. He said grace for all of them.

"Well, how is everyone, and especially my birthday girl?" Mr. Madison asked.

"I don't want to have a birthday, Daddy. Except now that you're here, it will be better." Marlee still hadn't come out of her slump.

"How did you get here so quickly? Did you drive all night?" Mrs. Madison asked her husband.

"Just about," he answered. "I drove almost straight through last night and figured if I didn't stop for anything but coffee all day, I could make it in time. I'm sorry I won't be much company tonight, kids. After this great meal, I'm going to hit the shower. And if you don't mind, Jenna Lee, I'll be off to bed, but—"

"It's okay, Dad. Get your sleep. We know you're tired," Park said.

"Yeah, Daddy, I'm just glad you got home safe," Marlee added.

"Marlee, here's what I'm thinking. How about tomorrow the three of us get up and out early for some fishing?" her dad asked.

"Oh, I'd love to!" Marlee exclaimed. She loved any time she got to spend with her dad. "I bet I catch more fish than you, Park."

"No way, Sport! I'll beat you, hands down," he countered, using the pet name he called his sister.

"How about I pack a picnic lunch and meet you there at noontime? I'll make your favorite peanut butter and butter sandwiches, Marlee," Mrs. Madison suggested.

"With real butter?" Marlee asked.

"Of course. How about going for a swim afterward? I'll have to be home in time to fix your special dinner, but we can spend the afternoon together, all four of us."

Marlee loved her mother's suggestion. She was glad her birthday came during the summer so she could spend her whole birthday celebrating. Parker's birthday was February 28, so he had to be in school on his birthday unless it fell on a weekend. Her dad tried to make it home for each family member's birthday. He was a long-haul trucker and spent a lot of time on the road. Her mom worked part-time at

Miss Belle's, and now that Park was sixteen, he had to work too, even if it was just part-time doing people's lawns. She knew she only had a few more years to be lazy over the summer break.

After everyone turned in for the night, Marlee lay in bed, thinking about the trip in the morning. Fishing! See, Dad wasn't making her change now that she would be thirteen. Maybe it wouldn't be so bad after all. She fell asleep before finishing that thought, and before she knew it, the alarm rang, and she had to get up and dressed for her fishing trip. At the last moment, she remembered to wear her bathing suit under her clothes.

They had a grand time, and Marlee thought it was one of her best birthdays ever. Mom had packed a super picnic and true to form, Marlee caught the most fish, five to her brother's four. Her dad only caught two. She wasn't surprised when she looked over and found him napping.

Marlee didn't know how he did it. Driving mile after mile would bore her to death. She didn't know how she would stay awake. Even now, if they took long trips in the car, Marlee slept most of the way. She knew her dad often ran on empty and too often pushed himself past where he should have. Marlee knew there were new limits on driving time, but she was sure her dad frequently pushed past them, especially if he was headed home.

Sure enough, her mom gave her a beautiful sweater, which she would wear the first chilly day back to school. Her mom had also made her an awesome purse to carry to school. She got a silver charm bracelet, which had been handed down to her from her mom's grandmother. Park gave her a three-pack of ChapSticks with summertime flavors like watermelon and mango. And she was surprised that her dad gave her a new dress. Though Marlee was not overly fond of dresses, she knew she would proudly wear it to church on Sunday and also on the first day back to school.

The rest of the summer vacation was ticking by alarmingly fast. Marlee knew she didn't have many days left to enjoy her leisure. She thought about the future when she would have to work during summer instead of being a layabout. She wanted to work at Miss Belle's, baking pies. That was the job Marlee really wanted. Miss Belle baked them fresh daily, and they were world-famous. Why, even a couple of state senators had been in to try them out.

She closed her eyes after staring all morning at the clouds in the sky. She had been picking out all the shapes she could identify. Somehow, she drifted off to sleep and was awakened by a few cold raindrops on her cheeks. She quickly raced home and up to her room. She looked at her calendar and crossed off another summer day. She was dismayed that this was her last Friday. Monday was the first day of school.

Besides bringing a mountain of schoolwork, the first day of school signaled the beginning of the big event. Every year, the town of Christmas put on a festival to celebrate the birth of the Baby Jesus, and it was the best-attended event for the Christmas season in the four-state region. When school began, so did the planning committees.

She didn't blame the town, it brought thousands of visitors, and she knew everyone could use the extra money. This year marked the 150th Annual Christmas Festival, so it was destined to be a special event.

Marlee had no idea what role she would play in making it so. She was about to embark on an adventure that would, not only change her life, but the lives of everyone in her hometown.

Chapter 2

Jem

Jem Jordan couldn't stop thinking about ways he could make money. He'd already taken his meager collection of comic books and ball cards into a comic shop in Henderson. Jem was hoping to get the amount he needed but fell way short. But he felt lucky to be given a hundred dollars. It seemed he owned a couple of valuable rookie cards, and apparently one of his comics was a rare error edition that made it valuable. The comic store owner was helpful. Jem ducked into the store while his mom had an appointment, and it didn't take a long time to haggle over the price. Jem didn't want his mother to know what he was doing. It wasn't so much that it would spoil his surprise, he just knew she wouldn't want him to do what he was doing.

Jem figured he was the man of the house even though he was only thirteen. He usually took care of his nine-year-old sister, Gracie, after school so his mother wouldn't have to pay a babysitter. Jem couldn't remember his father. He was five when his dad just up and left, took off just like that. In all the years since, there hadn't been a phone call, birthday card, or Christmas present and no money for his mom. That's what hurt the most. He hated to see his mom have to work so hard.

But boy could she bake! No one made better cakes, cookies, muffins, tarts, pastries, donuts, or scones. You name it, and she could bake it. Her lifelong dream was to open her own bakeshop, but she had to settle for baking the occasional wedding or birthday cake. She worked for Dr. Millman and was quite accomplished at that, too. Dr.

Millman still said he thanked the Lord for the day Elisabeth Jordan showed up to work for him. He did the doctoring, and she ran the office, and he often joked that he had the easier job.

For the past several years, his mom participated in the town's Christmas festival bake sale. She had come to rely on the money she made selling her baked goods. That meant between Thanksgiving and Christmas, his mother was busy baking nights and weekends. Last month, the oven started overheating, and Sam Caldwell from the H & M said he didn't think it could be fixed. It dated to the 1950s, and they didn't make parts for it anymore. The only way to fix it was to find a stove just like it with that part still working. *Good luck to that!* Jem thought. When he saw that his mother was near to tears, he vowed to do anything he could to get her a new stove.

He'd seen one at Lowes in Henderson for around six hundred dollars, so now he had to find a way to get the five hundred dollars he still needed. He didn't own anything else of value. He'd even gone to the bank to see if he could get a loan, but Mr. Bedminster, the bank president, said banks don't loan money unless you are eighteen. Mr. Bedminster sympathized with Jem. He would have lent him the money himself, but he just had a new addition to his family and was paying the hospital every spare cent he had.

Mrs. Hudson, his history teacher, called his name twice. "Jem Jordan, bring yourself back down to this classroom and get the fairy dust out of your pockets!" The class chuckled as Mrs. Hudson always used the oddest expressions. They all turned to see what Jem was doing.

He straightened himself up in his chair. "Sorry, Mrs. Hudson," he mumbled.

"You're to be the shepherd this year, Jem. You know what that means. You'll have to make arrangements with Mr. Bascombe to learn how to shepherd his sheep into town."

Jem realized what an honor it was to participate in the live manger scene on Nativity Night. This was more than just a live manger scene. It required him to shepherd a couple of sheep from Bascombe's farm to the Town Square where the manger scene was always set up. Jem knew that was a big responsibility, and he wasn't sure he could spare the time. Then he thought Mr. Bascombe might have some chores or small jobs he could do. That would mean giving up his Saturdays to work, but he was okay with that if it meant getting closer to his six-hundred-dollar goal.

Jem thought if he could find someone to loan him a bike, he could make his way between school, chores, and Bascombe's farm a lot faster than if he had to walk.

All this daydreaming made this last class speed by, and before he knew it, he was out the door and on his way home.

"Marlee! Patrick!" he shouted when he saw his friends ahead.

"What's up, Jem?" Marlee asked as they stopped to let him catch up.

"Do either of you guys have a bike I can borrow between now and Christmas?" he asked them.

Marlee thought about her old bike, which she had just put away for the winter when Patrick said, "Yeah, I have one you can use. I got it a couple of years ago, but you know me, I'm not much for bike riding."

"Yeah, we know," Marlee added. "It doesn't have a calculator tied to the handlebars."

"Not funny," Patrick said smiling.

"Can I come by your place and get it now?" Jem asked.

"Why do you need a bike?" Marlee questioned. "If you didn't ride one all summer, why are you starting now?"

"There's stuff I got to do, and riding is faster than walking," Jem answered her.

"What stuff?" Marlee asked. Jem could see she was going to be persistent.

"Yeah, I want to know what you're going to do on my bike," Patrick added. He didn't really care why Jem needed to borrow it, but he thought he would lend support to Marlee's inquisition.

"Tell us, Jem. You can't lead sheep riding on a bike," Marlee stated.

Jem thought it was going to be easy to borrow a bike, but now he had clearly raised Marlee's curiosity.

"You swear not to say anything? It's got to be a surprise. I don't want my mom to know."

"I have no reason to tell your mother anything as long as you're not going to harm yourself," Marlee assured him.

Even though she and Jem were the same age, Marlee treated him as a younger brother.

"Well, you know how much my mom counts on the money she gets from the festival bake sale," he started to tell them.

"Yeah, and you know how much we count on her bringing her baked goods, but what's that got to do with a bike?" Marlee said, even more curious.

"The oven on our stove isn't working right, and it can't be fixed. I have to find a way to buy her a new stove." Jem told them.

"But they're hundreds of dollars! How are you going to get that kind of money?" Marlee exclaimed.

Jem thought Marlee had a point. When he said it out loud, it did sound farfetched. Maybe he was kidding himself, but he wasn't ready to give up on his idea just yet.

"I already got a hundred dollars. I took my comics and ball cards into Henderson and sold them," he said with some determination back in his voice.

"You're still a long way off. How can you get the rest of that kind of money? Hey, I've got an idea. Why don't you borrow ours?" Marlee said, thinking this was the perfect solution.

"How am I going to get your stove over to my house?" Jem quizzed.

"No, silly. I mean your mom can come over to our house to do her baking. My mom doesn't use our oven that often. Besides, she's at Miss Belle's all the time."

"Marlee, are you sure your mom won't mind? I'll let my mom know, but I'm still going to try to earn the money I need. She'll be glad for the offer, but I know she won't want to impose for too long." Jem felt a little relief as he wasn't sure how successful his plan was going to be. At least this way his mom would still be able to bake.

"Okay, so what's your plan?" Patrick joined in the conversation. "You still haven't told us."

"I'm going to see if there are some chores or some kind of work out at Mr. Bascombe's farm, and I'll ask anyone else I can think of. I'll tell them I am willing to work every Saturday, sunup to sundown," Jem explained.

"Wow, that's a lot of work. But who's going to pay a kid that kind of money to do chores?" Marlee asked.

Jem thought she had a way of getting to the point, and it wasn't always encouraging.

"Oh, Jem, don't look like that. We'll think of something. Don't worry. I am a Madison, and we're not easily defeated. I'm even getting the hang of being thirteen. And you know, Mrs. Hudson picked me to be Mary this year, and you know what that means."

"Nobody believes in that Christmas wish stuff anymore," Patrick said. "This is the twenty-first century you know."

"Well, you never know, do you? I don't know how anybody can know for sure anyway. Miracles do happen." And with that, Marlee turned off to go to Belle's and Beaus, sure she would find her mother already there.

CHAPTER 3

Miss Belle

Belle Rose Atkins was not young anymore, and today, she was especially aware of it. Running her cafe from six in the morning until nine at night was finally catching up to her. Sure, she had help now, two cooks and two wait staff, but that didn't keep Belle out of the kitchen when it got a little slow or out front when it was unusually busy. Belle just loved people, and she just loved working.

She lived in the rooms above the cafe, which was convenient and saved time. And she had plenty of time on her hands now that she had no family or rather, now that she had no family left. She was done pining for the grandchildren she would never have and considered each and every child in Christmas as one of her own.

Her only son, Frank Junior, had been killed in the first Gulf War twenty-seven years ago, and husband, Frank, died in Vietnam. Her two beaus, she thought, as she looked over to the far wall where she had hung their photos, medals, and memorial flags. She named her cafe Belle's and Beaus because she believed it belonged to them, too.

Frankie was just a baby when she lost Frank. He had come home for what turned out to be his last time, and she was always grateful that he had seen his son before heading back to 'Nam. It wasn't too many months later that he was gone.

Over the years, she pushed that memory away from her as often as it arose and concentrated on raising Frankie as a widow. She never remarried. *Can't replace what can't be replaced*, she thought. She knew there would never be another love in her life because nothing could touch the love she had already known. Besides, she had the Lord and knew Jesus would be a true husband to her in her widowhood and a father to her fatherless son.

It was not without a great deal of trepidation that she waved goodbye to Frankie when he followed in his father's footsteps and joined the Marines. He was six months into his last deployment when the dreaded chaplain visit came. Belle nearly died from the heartbreak, at least she wished for it plenty of times. But her parents were still alive then, and she knew they depended on her, so she moved back to Christmas and dug in and got through the worst of it. Belle wasn't sure if they didn't help her more than she helped them. There were a lot of tears and a lot of prayers, and she thanked the Lord every day for carrying her through the terrible ordeal.

After her parents died, she sold their home and bought the cafe. It had been the right move, and she felt very blessed. She never wanted much, certainly not riches, as she'd already lost everything of real value in her life. She knew that Frank and Frankie and her parents weren't really lying in the town cemetery, and when it was her time, she'd have a grand reunion in heaven. Belle's only wishes were that the cafe would make enough to keep running, and it would enable her set aside enough funds to carry her through the rest of her days. At sixty-nine, she knew she couldn't work forever, at least not at her current pace, but hoped she had at least another ten good years.

She truly enjoyed the years she had owned her business. At first, she could only afford to be open for breakfast and lunch, and back then she did it all by herself. Eventually, she felt confident she could afford to pay someone to help, and plenty of times, she really had to scrape by to do so. She was rather used to doing without if she had to.

But one day, a couple of truckers came into town and stopped by her place, and ever since then, she had been doing reasonably well. The word had gotten out that it was worth a fifteen-mile trip off the interstate to stop by the Christmas Church Cafe as her place became known. It was not just the food they came for but the company as well.

Over the years, Belle got to know all about the drivers, their families, and their trials. She promised to pray for each and every one of them. After a while, her list became so long that she just prayed for "the list." She kept the prayer requests tacked up on the wall and every now and then, she could mark through one with PRAISE in big block letters. Jesus was just always a part of Belle's conversation, and no one was more excited than she to find out when one of her customers had indeed taken Jesus into his heart and life.

She wiped down the counter for what seemed like the hundredth time. This was the lull after lunch but before dinner. She had just finished putting the last of the day's pies into the oven. Martha Cooper, her morning cook, had left for the day and Jackson Perch, her evening cook, had just arrived. She knew Jenna Lee Madison would be coming soon, too.

Jackson was a wiz in the kitchen. He was about her age and had resumed work after his wife died. They had retired from their restaurant business in Henderson; sold it to a young couple. They had planned to do some traveling before settling down into retirement, but Mariah got sick. They had a son in Atlanta, and a daughter somewhere in North Carolina, and Jackson had six grandchildren that were the loves of his life. After Mariah's unexpected death and with his children moved away, Jackson decided he needed to work. He enjoyed the part-time hours, especially in the evening because Jackson said that his happier times were in the daytime while the sun was shining. When the sun set, the darkness of the day matched the darkness of his sorrow, and that's when Jackson decided he needed to stay busy. He could work hard at Belle's and go home and fall right into bed.

Belle shared her own story with him and told him how much Jesus wanted to help him, too. He finally gave in and "gave way to the Holy Spirit" and let Jesus come into his heart. He still remembers the fine celebration they had, Miss Belle going all out so he would remember that day as being the first day of his new life.

Just then, Jenna Lee stepped through the door. "And how are you this fine day, Miss Belle?" she asked.

"Why I'm just fine and dandy, Jenna Lee." This was their routine every day that Jenna Lee came to work.

Just then, Marlee burst through the front door. Without looking to see who else was in the room, she launched into her announcement.

"Mom! Mom!" she said with more than her usual amount of excitement.

"Marlee, mind your manners," her mother said frowning. She nodded her head toward Miss Belle.

Belle had already stopped what she was doing as Marlee turned to acknowledge her presence.

"Sorry. Hey, Miss Belle." Without pausing for breath, Marlee continued.

"I got selected to be Mary and Park is Joseph and Liam and Patrick are kings, along with Hudson and Gracie's gonna be the angel and oh, Jem's going to be the shepherd. And, oh yes, I promised him that his mom could come over and use our oven anytime she needs to bake. Is that okay? I hope it's okay 'cause I already promised."

"Marlee, slow down. I'm sorry, Belle. I'm sure Marlee doesn't mean to be rude." Jenna Lee emphasized this last statement and looked at Marlee in such a way that Marlee knew she was being rude and that she should apologize.

"I'm sorry, Miss Belle. It's just that I'm not usually this excited."

Belle laughed to herself because Marlee was always this excited.

"It's just, well you know what it means to be picked to be Mary," Marlee trailed off, looking from her mother to Miss Belle and back to her mother again.

"Now, Marlee, I don't want you getting all worked up over the notion that there is going to be a wish granted just because you get to hold the Baby Jesus figure. That's superstitious nonsense, and I don't want you getting carried away," her mother admonished her.

"But, Mom, it's true. Lots of things have happened. Liam said when his mom played Mary, she wished for Mrs. Hatcher to have a baby. And the following Christmas, she did, even though she and her husband had been trying for over ten years. And two years ago, Ashley was Mary, and her best friend's mom had been sick for months, bedridden even. She prayed for her to get well, and she did, and last year, Hayden was Mary, and well, I'm not sure what Hayden wished for, but I'll ask her, I'm sure it came true."

"Marlee, catch your breath. The year I played Mary, I had my wish, but I knew it wouldn't happen, and it didn't. Lots of people have wishes that come true, and lots don't. The ones that do are probably just coincidences," her mother said.

"She's right, Sweetie." Belle chimed in. "We don't really need wishes when we have the right to bring our prayers right into God's throne room and present them to him. The Bible says he'll give us the desires of our heart, but we must accept his will because he knows what's best for us. Sometimes, the things we wish for wouldn't be good for us, even if we thought they would be."

"But that's why you can't wish for yourself or someone in your family. It has to be for someone else, and you have to believe it will come true or it won't. Maybe that's why it didn't work for you, Mom. I'm going to think long and hard about my wish. I want it to be the perfect Christmas wish."

"Well, don't get too carried away. I don't want you to be disappointed if it doesn't come true. And think about what Miss Belle said. Prayers are worth investing in. Besides, I don't think Jesus would like it if he thought a figure of himself as a baby was considered a 'good luck' charm. Now I've got to get to work. Your dinner is in the fridge."

Their dinner was always in the fridge, Marlee thought as she left for home. She had to admit she wasn't as excited as she had been when she arrived. Marlee thought her mother would be happy to hear her good news.

Dad, she'd tell her dad! He'd be excited for her. She wasn't sure when he would be home. Maybe he knew someone who had the Christmas wish come true. He'd lived his whole life in Christmas. She'd ask him the first chance she got.

Okay, Mom, wait 'til you see. This is going to be one spectacular Christmas festival. I'm going to be Mary and hold the Baby Jesus figure and make a Christmas wish!

With that, she took off at a run, her spirits revived.

After Marlee left, Jenna Lee looked at Belle and shrugged.

"You have to admit, Jenna Lee, she is a spunky one. Only your Marlee could be that excited to be Mary. Just wait until she realizes how cold and dark it is around here on December 24. She might not be so excited when she realizes what she's in for," Belle chuckled.

With that, she gave Mrs. Madison a hug and left her to her work. Still, Jenna Lee was worried. If there was any truth to the legend, she had no doubt Marlee would be in the center of it. Her daughter was one of a kind, no doubt about that. She just wondered what kind of trouble might lie ahead if Marlee got too caught up in wishes and legends.

CHAPTER 4

Marlee's Lesson

Marlee had settled into school and was finding that there wasn't much difference in being thirteen after all. *I guess it's all in how you look at it*, she thought. Marlee was enjoying most of her classes, but history was much harder than last year. She was troubled by some of the things she was learning about.

Though the mornings started out cool, the afternoons were still mild enough that she could enjoy being outside. Marlee hated the arrival of cold weather. Fall was coming soon enough, and the temperatures would start growing cooler. When daylight savings ended, the days would get dark earlier in the evening. She'd no longer have the freedom that daylight provided and knew she would have to be indoors more, something she really hated.

She decided to stop at Miss Belle's on her way home since this was a night her mom wasn't scheduled to work. Marlee was pondering a problematic topic in history.

"Miss Belle, was Christmas ever segregated?"

Belle looked up as Marlee entered, never really surprised at what came out of that girl's thoughts.

"Why on earth would you be thinking about that?" Miss Belle asked her.

"It's in our history books. I just wondered. I have to admit, I don't understand it at all."

"Folks in Christmas had too many other worries to be concerned with. When folks are hurting, no one pays attention to what color skin you have." Miss Belle smiled. In many ways, Marlee was "an innocent," but on the other hand, she was sharp as a tack.

"Did you ever experience prejudice?" Marlee asked her, hoping she would say no, as Marlee loved Miss Belle and wondered why everyone else wouldn't also.

"Well, I suppose I've had my share," Belle said, remembering a few unpleasant events in her life. "But I never paid it any mind. Prejudice is the devil's doing. I prefer to concentrate on what God is doing."

"But people are talking about how Christians are responsible for some of the most horrible things in history!" Marlee was clearly perturbed by this thought.

"Well, those were Christians in name only. That's the devil's doing also."

"What do you mean?" Marlee asked.

Marlee always came to Miss Belle when she had to solve a difficult problem. Miss Belle knew more about the Bible than anyone she'd ever met, and she knew she would have an answer for her if there were one. She never met anyone smarter than Miss Belle.

"Well, Marlee, ask yourself this about those horrible things, would Jesus have done them?"

"No way!"

"Just so. People can call themselves Christians 'til they're blue in the face. Saying so doesn't make it so. The Bible says you identify Christians by their fruit. You know, goodness, kindness, patience, and self-control. If you come in Jesus's name, you better be coming in love. There's just no other way to treat people."

"Miss Belle, how long has your family lived here?"

"In Christmas? My great-great-grandmother came here after she was freed by President Lincoln. That was back right after word got out that gold had been discovered and the town became a boomtown. She worked as a laundress since the men didn't have anyone to do their laundry. She also did a lot of sewing and mending and eventually was able to become a dressmaker when the boom ended. She was a smart one, she was. Some folks took advantage of her, but in the end, she owned her own shop. Then she met and married my great-great-grandfather, and here I am. Though you know, I lived away from Christmas while my husband was in the military. I moved back here after he died."

"So why do people call themselves Christians if they really aren't?"

"Well, Marlee, your question is one for the ages so to speak. I guess there's not one answer to that. Sometimes, people just don't know the real meaning of the term. For example, how do you suppose you can call yourself a Christian, yet you don't go to church, and you've never read the Bible?"

"I never thought of it that way. I guess you would want to know at least what you were supposed to believe." Marlee couldn't remember a time when she didn't attend church, and reading the Bible was as important as eating a meal.

"Right you are. But some people think being an American and being a Christian are the same thing, and that's just not so. And some think they must be a Christian if they're not something else, like Buddhist or Muslim, but that just isn't so. You've been to Sunday school long enough to know how a person becomes a Christian because you aren't born a Christian, even if your parents were Christians at the time of your birth."

"You have to want to be a Christian. It means recognizing you're a sinner to start with." Marlee didn't have to think hard for the answer. She had already accepted Jesus as her Lord and Savior. Miss Belle was there at her baptism service. "But you know, to tell you the truth, Miss Belle, having Jesus as Savior is a whole lot easier than having him as Lord."

Miss Belle knew there was a lot of truth in that statement.

Marlee continued. "So, I know I want to go to heaven when I die. I confess that I am a sinner, and Jesus, who was perfect as a human being, takes my sin and gives me his perfection because only perfect people can go to heaven. Mama would for sure tell you I'm a long way from being perfect. Sin must be punished, and I deserve to die. I won't if I accept his gift. It's like going to court and being declared innocent even when you know you are guilty."

"Well said, Marlee! You are destined for great things with that knowledge. But what about Jesus being your Lord?" Miss Belle knew Marlee had her priorities in the right order and wished all of America's young people could have a similar vision, something she prayed for nightly.

"Miss Belle, I'm having a lot of trouble with that part."

"You are not alone, my dear. We all struggle with that part," Belle said. She knew this was the universal problem for all Christians, even the Apostle Paul struggled with it.

"What's hard about it, Miss Belle, is that I'm not sure we know how to submit. In America, it's of the people, by the people and for the people. We never had a king, and we're proud of being self-sufficient. We govern ourselves, and we're taught not to rely on anyone else in life. I know my granddaddy used to tell me, 'You're a Madison, we forge our own way.' But letting Jesus be Lord means I have to stop forging *my* way and start forging *his* way. That's the hard part because I keep forgetting, and I just do it my way all the time."

"Do you think that you have to stop being you in any way? Because God sure broke the mold when he made you!" Miss Belle chuckled.

"I think we're all unique. Everyone is one of a kind. Even identical twins are different from each other. That's what's wonderful about each and every life," Marlee answered her.

"I wish more young people like you realized that. You are so very wise to understand that, Marlee. Young people need to recognize how unique they are just the way they're made and stop trying to change themselves into something else, something that won't make them any happier, and certainly won't make them more valuable as a person. Don't try to change the outside because it's the inside person that matters. Does each person realize God brought them into the world to be a special person and have a special purpose? If you know God made you just the way you are, don't try to improve on what he created, and dress it up differently. Accept that you are just the way God made you and embrace all of your uniqueness as you are.

"You asked about segregation, and I said prejudice was the devil's doing. Everybody wants some reason to think they're better in some way than someone else. Prejudice comes in all forms, not just race. But nothing on the outside makes a lick of difference. Not white or black nor any color, not if you're skinny like you or fat like me, not your height or your eye color or your hair color, not even male or female. What matters is your inside, your heart, and your soul. And you must address your sin. If you don't do something about it, you're doomed. You have to resolve the sin issue while you're alive. If you're dead, it's too late. And like you say, only perfect people go to heaven, and there is not one perfect person who ever lived except Jesus," Miss Belle finished.

"You have to trade your sin for Jesus's perfection. That's the only way you can go to heaven," Marlee said.

"Yes, Marlee. Whether you like it or not, that is the only way to get to heaven. Not because we say so, but because Jesus said so. And praise Jesus, he is willing to do it. I'll say it again, Marlee. You are destined for great things!"

'Well, right now I'll just settle for passing Mrs. Hudson's history class."

"I hear she assigned your whole class a project on the history of this town."

"Yes, I've decided I'll study the Baby Jesus figure, you know, how it got here, how old it is, the history behind it. I'm sure Miss Pemberton will be a great help. She knows everything about this town. I also want to find out more about the legend. Maybe I can prove it's true. I hope there's some truth behind it. I don't think legends get started for no reason at all."

"That sounds like a fine project to me. Have you thought of your wish yet?" The twinkle in Miss Belle's eyes let Marlee know she was humoring her. She knew Miss Belle loved her like she was her own grandchild and she loved Miss Belle back.

"Not yet," she replied.

Marlee had been contemplating her Christmas wish ever since she found out she'd be Mary, but she still had no idea what to wish for.

"Well, you still have plenty of time," Miss Belle said. She wished something good would happen for Marlee this Christmas. There was no child with a better heart. Let her have her dreams, there was still plenty of time before she had to face the way the real world worked.

"You know this is the town's 150th festival, Marlee," Belle continued.

"I know! That's why it has to be special this year."

"You know what else it means? You have a hundred and forty-nine wishes to research." Miss Belle looked at Marlee whose smile suddenly changed to a frown.

"Oh no. I never thought of it that way. That's going to be a lot of work."

"You let me know what you find out. If it's true, I can always change my mind," Belle told her.

Belle loved Marlee's visits. They always brought a smile, especially to her heart.

"Miss Belle, do you need someone to make sure your pies are fit to eat this evening?" Marlee's visits also brought a lot of laughter and this time was no exception.

"I'm sure someone needs to taste them. Come on back here, and let's see."

"And, Miss Belle?"

"Yes, Marlee?"

"You're not fat."

"Oh, Marlee," she said laughing. "You are a treasure."

Marlee turned to follow her back to the kitchen, not sure what it was she said that was so funny.

CHAPTER 5

Miss Pemberton and Jedediah

Miss Pemberton tried to bring order by banging the gavel down hard, as hard as an eighty-two-year-old woman could. She kept missing the sound block, the small round block of wood she was trying to hit. She caught the side of it, which caused it to jump then did it again with the same result. The third time it tipped on its side and rolled to the floor. Miss Pemberton had a funny look on her face as she watched it disappear. She couldn't bend over to reach it, so she tried calling for order, but over the din of conversation, no one could hear her. The adults in the room were too distracted to notice her, but all the kids did, and they couldn't stop laughing. Mayor Donnelly finally turned to see Miss Pemberton's distress and saw she was scowling.

"Are you ready to get started?" he asked her.

"Have been," she said in a huff.

Miss Pemberton was the town's historian and librarian. She also was the guardian of the town's historical records and artifacts. Over her lifetime, she had assembled them into a small museum. They had started saving these records in the 1800s when some enterprising soul with enough foresight realized the day might come when there would be some interest in studying the town's beginnings. They had kept all the early land registers and local newspaper accounts of town events. There were plenty of ledgers, which Miss Pemberton had identified and labeled and placed neatly on bookshelves located on the second floor of the library. She also had all the records of the Town Festival Planning Committee, something her grandmother had started over a hundred years ago when the festival began to attract folks from beyond the town of Christmas.

Miss Pemberton had lived in Christmas all her life. She never married, though she came close once, but the young man turned out to be a gold hunter and was only courting Miss Pemberton for her historical knowledge. He gave up on finding the gold and on her when he realized Miss Pemberton couldn't help him with any clues. Miss Pemberton had spent nearly all her life explaining to treasure hunters that if she knew where Jedediah Christmas Smith had hidden his gold, she would not be a librarian.

She lived in the same house she grew up in, having inherited it from her parents after they died. Her father had been the president of the Christmas Bank & Trust and had left her well enough off that she could dedicate herself to the preservation of the town's history.

When the only saloon in town went out of business, Miss Pemberton's mother secured the building for a library. They brought over an accumulation of books from the basement in Town Hall. Miss Pemberton had studied the Dewey Decimal System by correspondence course and organized all the books officially into a real library. Over the many years since, she was able to purchase several cartons of books each year with the small library budget that came from the state. Miss Pemberton had petitioned the state legislature many times to increase the budget and had often been successful. Though most people used the library in Henderson because it had Internet service, Miss Pemberton was proud that she had obtained all the research materials needed by students as they made their way through the local school system as well as lots of the best literature to read for pleasure.

Since there were more boxes of records than she could have imagined a small-town like Christmas generating, there were records she still had not organized or cross-referenced. Miss Pemberton thought they should have invented computers earlier. Were they available when she was younger, she could have made great use of one, but by the time they were, Miss Pemberton thought she was too old to learn. She still did things by hand using three by five cards and notebooks. She had been able to salvage a few display cases when local businesses excessed them, and you could see Miss Pemberton's neatly printed labels on the items she had selected for display. Most of the people who visited the museum were either people interested in local history or they were out-of-towners who still came annually to discover gold. The second group always left empty-handed.

Miss Pemberton thought it almost sacred to be allowed to handle the few items left behind by the town's founder, Jedediah Christmas Smith. Smith came to the area over 150 years ago, and as legend had it, found a small fortune in gold. Over the years as the legend grew, so did the amount of gold he left behind, and this was what brought treasure hunters to Christmas.

Smith came alone and had no family. Those who asked were told, "Didn't have none coming into the world and won't have none when I leave." What little he would say was that he was left on the steps of a small church in Virginia on the day of his birth, Christmas 1829. Pastor Ezekiel Smith and his wife, Margaret, were stunned when they heard a baby crying outside their door. Because they had no children of their own, they decided to raise him themselves, even though both were getting on in years at the time. So, they named him Jedediah Christmas, Jedediah being the name of the pastor's father. By the time he was twelve, both of them had died, and Jedediah had to make his way in the world.

Margaret and Ezekiel gave him a strict upbringing in the Bible and taught him the "Mysteries and Wonders of God." Jedediah couldn't have been loved more had Margaret been his real mother. After he saw both parents buried, he left his hometown to make a living.

Jedediah was a frugal man, no doubt owing to Margaret's upbringing. Over time, he was able to earn his keep, scraping by trouble from time to time. Jedediah never married as he thought having a family wouldn't do with his way of life. He roamed from place to place and never thought there would ever be a place where he would settle down.

But that was when his circumstances changed, and he found himself up in the mountains of eastern Kentucky. One day, while he was hunting and trapping, he found gold.

He didn't get as excited as most men do when they get gold fever but instead looked back to all the old Bible lessons from Margaret and asked himself why God would bless him in that way.

So, he started the town of Christmas, and in 1868, he started an annual Christmas celebration. He had "found the Lord" several years before that, and since he and the Lord shared the same birthday, what better way to honor him than to celebrate his Advent.

Over time as the town grew, so did the festival. Sometime in the mid-1950s, when there was a little more prosperity in the area, and the roads had improved allowing people to travel, and gas stations popped up in more places, the townspeople of Christmas noticed more and more visitors coming to town to participate each year.

The town started expanding the festival, and it now ran for nearly two weeks. It culminated in the live recreation of the nativity, which they called Nativity Night. This recreation wasn't just a live manger scene like it was in the beginning; it was a pageant where Mary rode a donkey, Joseph by her side as they traveled to "Bethlehem." They also had three kings (with horses for camels for obvious reasons) and a shepherd who herded sheep to the manger site.

The only time Jedediah ever left Christmas was when he had traveled to Rome to see where they executed Peter and Paul. He brought back a life-sized Baby Jesus figure carved from wood and beautifully painted. He said it was over three hundred years old and had cost a pretty penny.

Now the town had its special Baby Jesus to use each year, and Jedediah asked that the tradition continue after he was gone. He hoped everyone would celebrate the birth of the Savior and would want to participate in the community celebration for as long as the town remained. One of the last things he had done in his life was to beautify the Town Square and place a bronze plaque in the center to commemorate what he had started in 1868, and it read: The Heart of Christmas is the Christ Child 25 December 1868.

The town honored his wishes, and this year would be the 150th anniversary of that first celebration.

Miss Pemberton looked over the room as the conversations died away. "Welcome ladies and gentlemen, and children, to our first planning meeting for the 150th anniversary celebration of our Christmas festival!"

The room applauded more because she had said this in a tone of voice meant to elicit applause rather than from their excitement at being there. Most everyone just wanted to get on with it as it was Saturday, and they had lots to do at home.

"Yes indeed, this year will be a special anniversary. As you know for 149 years, this town has had our Nativity Night in Town Square with the same Baby Jesus figure held by 149 young ladies chosen to be Mary. Congratulations to Marlee Madison who is our Mary this year."

The audience applauded again. Marlee tried to sink into her seat, but her mother made her raise her arm so everyone could see where she was sitting.

"I understand that Mrs. Hudson has assigned her history class to prepare a special project on the history of this town, and we will be displaying the student's work prominently in the library."

Oh no, Marlee moaned silently. *Mrs. Hudson never told us that. I'm doomed*, she thought. Marlee realized this was now going to take more Saturdays than she wanted to give up. She thought about the boxes of dusty papers she would have to sort through.

"Now I've made a preliminary list of all the events. I've put your name next to each event if you chaired that committee last year. I want to have our next meeting in two weeks at this same time, so please bring any changes with you. This year, we have to relocate both the bake sale and the craft sale as they've outgrown their current locations. So, bakers, you will be moving to the elementary school and crafters, you will be in the gymnasium of the middle school instead of in the cafeteria. Ben Johnson," she called as she gazed over the crowd trying to locate him. "Ben, I understand you have volunteered to be our Santa this year. Sadly, Mr. Thompson moved away from Christmas last spring, but I hear he is doing quite well at his nursing home in Henderson. I know quite a few of you have been over there to see him. Please wish him well from us and tell him how much we miss him.

"Ben, I am assuming your son Tim, do I see Tim? Yes, Tim, you are still in charge of getting Santa's Workshop ready. Does everyone know Tim? He will be our handyman if you need something."

Tim was a carpenter and something of a handyman and had already been out to the Workshop to start any necessary repairs. It was located in the center of a grove of trees on the outskirts of town. One of the highlights of the festival was the hay wagon they decorated to look like a sleigh. It was used to bring kids from town out to Santa's Workshop. With lights and silver bells hung on the tree branches, the grove looked like a beautiful wonderland at night.

"Please remember the Grand Illumination and get your lights hung in time. The more lights, the better," Miss Pemberton reminded them.

The Grand Illumination was the grand finale of the Festival and occurred after the "birth" of the baby. Right before midnight, the whole town went dark. The moments ticked by eerily until just after midnight when they played the sounds of a baby's cries on the loudspeaker. The angel climbed to the top of the manger and with a spotlight shining on her said, "Hosanna in the highest, Peace on Earth, Goodwill to all Men. Our Savior has been born." At that moment, everyone with a house or shop bordering Town Square, turned on their Christmas lights. The scene was glorious. That would be Marlee's final moment as Mary and, as she held the Baby Jesus figure, she would make her Christmas wish.

"Our town tree is scheduled to arrive on December 1, so there will be plenty of time to decorate it," Miss Pemberton continued. "We are still a few months away, but I would like to stress that time flies by so please everyone, do not procrastinate. And one more rule of mine, *have fun*! We expect a crowd of several thousand this year so be prepared but enjoy yourselves. We want to put on a pretty spectacular show, and we can't forget this is a special anniversary and sure to generate additional revenue for both you and the town. I want all our vendors to be particularly successful, so if you encounter any problem, let your team lead, the mayor, or me know right away. Remember, lots of visitors will be looking for unique gifts, so crafters and shop owners, take note. And let's hope they come with big appetites and a thirst for our goodies.

"The more you can decorate your businesses for Christmas, the better. We are also offering an ornament hunt for those of you who want to provide discount coupons. Let me know how many ornaments you each need as I am placing the order in another week."

Each of the shop owners who offered discounts would tape their coupons to these ornaments. Then they would be "hidden" around town for attendees to find and use.

Miss Pemberton looked over her notes. "Did I miss anything, Mayor? If that's it, everyone please proceed out to the hall and meet up with your team. Please try to volunteer for at least one team. Thank you all for coming. Those of you in the Nativity Night cast, please stay behind and see me for a few minutes."

Marlee got her instructions from Miss Pemberton, and on the way home went over them in her mind. After all, they weren't complicated. She knew how to ride a horse and figured riding a donkey wouldn't be much different.

Miss Pemberton kept all the costumes and props locked away in a closet on the second floor of the library. She also kept the Baby Jesus figure in its own box, and Marlee wouldn't be able to hold it until the first full dress rehearsal a week before the Festival began. All the cast were to meet after Thanksgiving for costume fittings. That gave Mrs. Stewart, who worked at the dry cleaner, plenty of time to make any adjustments. Marlee asked Miss Pemberton if she could see the Baby Jesus at that time, and Miss Pemberton said yes if she stayed after her fitting. Miss Pemberton planned to open the box herself to make sure the figure didn't need attention.

That night, Marlee had a strange dream. She found Jedediah Smith's gold, which had been hidden inside the Baby Jesus figure. When she woke the next morning, she wondered if such a thing were possible.

CHAPTER 6

Mr. Trumbull

Hiram Trumbull lived on the outskirts of town opposite where the main road entered from the Interstate. His home had once been the showplace in Christmas, but for years, it hadn't been kept up. The white paint on the clapboard siding had worn so badly that the house now looked gray. Weeds choked nearly all of the once beautiful rose gardens. The wind had blown the leaves into large piles around the wrought iron fence. There were shingles loose on the roof, and the porch sagged a bit.

All the kids in town thought the place was haunted and wouldn't go near it. The only thing past the house was Bascombe's farm so almost no one, except Mr. Bascombe and his farm hands, ever ventured out that way. Mr. Trumbull was ninety-two and a recluse, although he made a daily trip into town every Monday through Friday. He thought children were a nuisance. He went out of his way to avoid them and, short of thoroughly disliking them, he did chase them away if they dared venture onto his property.

He left his home promptly at 3:00 p.m. for his trips to town. On Mondays and Thursdays, he stopped into the H & M for groceries. He only bought a small amount. Anything more was too much for him to carry home. On Tuesdays and Wednesdays, he stopped into Belle's and Beaus for a piece of pie and hot coffee. Fridays would find him in the cemetery visiting his late wife and son. On these daily trips, he never spoke to anyone, even when someone said hello. His reply was a grunt and a nod of his head. He would tip his hat if it were a woman. He never responded in any way if it were a youngster.

His routine never changed. He always picked up the same items at the H & M, and it was a rare day indeed if he decided to try one of Miss Belle's new pies. Instead, he always chose apple on Tuesday and pecan on Wednesday.

Jem was riding Patrick's bike on his way to Bascombe's farm. He was daydreaming about just how much money he might be able to make. At the same time, he was trying to stay close to the curb but had to give up as there were too many piles of leaves in the way. Just as he swerved the bike from the street to the sidewalk, Mr. Trumbull stepped out of his gate, forcing Jem to twist the bike to the left to avoid hitting him. Mr. Trumbull did not see him until it was almost too late. Jem was unable to control the bike when the tire moved onto the grass, and he went down, bike and all.

"Don't you know how to look where you're going?" Mr. Trumbull said. He was never polite, and his old voice was hoarse and gravelly.

"I'm sorry, Mr. Trumbull. I didn't see you 'til the last second," Jem apologized.

Jem was looking over the bike, more concerned with it than either himself or Mr. Trumbull since he knew he couldn't have hurt the old gentleman. He couldn't afford to pay for repairs to the bike, and it would be a lot of trouble if he had to replace it.

He got himself untangled from the bike, and fortunately, he could see no damage.

"Are you all right?" Mr. Trumbull asked, finally conceding that the child might have injured himself, and he didn't want to have to be bothered calling the authorities to tend to him.

"I guess so," Jem said as he looked down and saw that he had skinned his elbow. "I don't care about me, but I borrowed this bike, and I can't afford for it to be damaged." He rubbed his elbow, and there was a small amount of blood. "I'm glad I didn't rip my pants. My mom would be so mad if I did. I only have a couple of other pairs, and I have to make them last."

He certainly didn't want to add another worry to his mother's load.

"All the more reason for you to look where you are going. I could have been killed." With that, Mr. Trumbull ended the conversation and continued on his way.

Jem couldn't take off fast enough, worried that Mr. Trumbull might turn around and give him an evil eye look. Jem dared not look back to see.

By the time he reached Mr. Bascombe's farm, he was out of breath. He planned to ask Mr. Bascombe if he could use some extra hands for a chore or two before he had to start practicing for Nativity Night. He found Mr. Bascombe cleaning out some stalls.

"Well, it's young Jeremy. I didn't expect you out this way so soon," Mr. Bascombe greeted him.

"I'm not here for Nativity Night. I, uh, I'm, uh, I'm." Jem was so nervous he couldn't figure how to phrase his question, so he just blurted it out. "Please, sir, do you have any chores I can do?"

"Chores, huh? Why would a young lad like you come out all this way to do chores? You can't be more than thirteen or fourteen."

"I'm thirteen, sir, but I'm stronger than I look, and I'll work hard," Jem promised.

"And just why do you need to work for me? Doesn't your mother keep you busy with chores at home? And what about your schoolwork?"

Mr. Bascombe kept working while they talked and barely looked at Jem.

"I was hoping I could come out here on Saturdays. I'm willing to work all day, sunup to sundown. I just really need the money, sir. Really," Jem said, hoping Mr. Bascombe wasn't deliberately avoiding him.

"Just how much money are we talking about?"

Mr. Bascombe thought Jem had no idea what working on a farm from sunup to sundown was like, but he was curious why any young man would be willing to come all this way to ask. He stopped shoveling and looked at Jem.

"I need five hundred dollars more. But any amount would help. Any amount."

Even to Jem's ears, his request sounded impossible, and Mr. Bascombe probably thought he was out of his mind.

"Five hundred dollars," Mr. Bascombe said thoughtfully, trying not to look amused.

What on earth did a child his age need with that kind of money? But then he thought about his childhood. Times had been tough for him growing up, and he was not too different from Jem, farming himself out to others to make a little money to help his family.

They nearly lost the farm when he was about Jem's age. That was the year his sister's best friend had been Mary, and shortly after Christmas, his dad received a letter from a bank in North Carolina. It seemed his grandfather had left a bank account when he died that no one knew about, and the bank had been looking for his next of kin for years. In the letter was a check for just over twelve hundred dollars, and it had been enough to save the farm.

"I got a field with a fence that needs repairing. You think you can replace some broken rails for me? I figure there are about a hundred of them, so I'll pay you a hundred dollars," Mr. Bascombe told him.

"Oh, Mr. Bascombe, that's great. I'll be here next Saturday right at sunup," Jem promised.

"Make sure you eat a hearty breakfast. You'll need it. Not easy work on a farm, you know."

Jem was on his return trip home when he had to pass by Mr. Trumbull's. He decided to ride on the other side of the street but slowed down to get a better look at the place. Mr. Trumbull was a mean old man, just like everyone said he was. Jem knew it was his fault, though, as he hadn't been looking where he was going.

He wanted to get home before sunset, and already the light was starting to fade. It did look haunted when there wasn't much light, he thought, but in the daylight it just looked rundown. There were other houses in Christmas that needed just as much attention.

Just then he thought he saw a curtain move slightly. That spooked him and sent a chill down his spine. He tried to convince himself that he had seen too many *Goosebumps* movies. Houses were not really haunted, and there was no such thing as an evil eye. Patrick didn't believe in that kind of stuff, and Patrick was the smartest kid in school.

Once again, he took off and rode as fast as he could to get home before it got dark. That night, Jem dreamed Mr. Trumbull was cracking a whip over him, making him put up fence rails faster and faster. Fortunately, when he awoke, the dream was forgotten. But now he had another plan.

The next day after school, Jem rode out to Mr. Trumbull's with a rake tied to the handlebars of the bike and a couple of large plastic leaf bags hanging out of his back pocket. It was no easy feat riding with a rake sticking out on both sides, and he must have looked a sight. He managed to pass everyone without hitting them. He hid around the corner waiting for Mr. Trumbull to leave his house. A few minutes passed, and he heard the gate opening and closing.

As soon as Mr. Trumbull was out of sight, Jem got right to work. He raked as fast as he could. When the pile of leaves was big enough, Jem shoveled them into the plastic bag. He was on his second bag when he realized it was time for Mr. Trumbull to return, so he grabbed the rake and the bags and took off, running around the corner back to his bike. No sooner had he got there than Mr. Trumbull came around the corner. Jem hoped he had remembered to close the gate all the way.

He waited long enough for Mr. Trumbull to disappear into his house before he felt safe enough to come out of his hiding place. On his way home, he dumped the leaves in the woods behind the high school because he didn't think he could manage for very long with a bag tied to each end of the rake.

Jem repeated this process for two more days, but there were so many leaves to rake he almost abandoned his plan. He found he was neglecting his homework, and his mom almost caught him one night when he had stayed up well past his bedtime to finish.

Saturday arrived, so Jem grabbed breakfast and took a few more pieces of toast with him and told his mom he was headed out to Bascombe's farm.

"Isn't it a bit early for that?" she asked.

She didn't think Jem needed to start practicing this early; it wasn't even Halloween yet.

"I want to get a head start," he replied.

He didn't want to tell his mother a lie, so technically, if he went into the sheep pen to get familiar with the sheep, it should count as practicing. After all, the sheep needed to get used to being around him, too. At least that is what Jem told himself.

"Don't be out after dark," his mother admonished.

"I won't, Mom, promise."

Jem thought about giving up another Saturday while the weather was still nice enough to be out with his friends, but lately, Marlee hadn't been around much anyway. *She really is wrapped up in this Christmas project stuff,* he thought to himself. *I haven't even started yet. What's the hurry,* he thought, *I still have plenty of time left.*

Mr. Bascombe wasn't kidding when he said the work was hard. Jem had only gotten about half the rails replaced. By the end of the day, his shoulders and back ached, and his fingers were full of splinters before he thought to ask Mr. Bascombe if he could borrow some gloves. He also decided he needed to wear boots the next time because sneakers didn't offer much protection against stepping in manure. As he rode home, all he wanted was a shower and supper, and in that order, even though he would have preferred to eat first. He hadn't brought anything for lunch, but he knew his mother would not let him sit at the table as stinky as he was. And he knew there was no way he could bring his shoes indoors.

His mom was in the kitchen when he walked in the door. "Where are your shoes?" she asked him as soon as he walked through the door.

How on earth did she know he wasn't wearing his shoes? he thought.

"You don't want them in the house, so I left them outside. I'll clean them in the morning." Who knew sheep made that much manure? He laughed, sure his mom didn't want to hear what he was thinking while she was fixing food.

"You look positively done in." She came out of the kitchen wiping her hands on a rag. "Are the sheep that hard to manage?"

"I was helping Mr. Bascombe with something, and it was more work than I thought."

"Well go on up and get your shower and send Gracie down here for me," she said.

The next morning, Jem retrieved his sneakers from the front stoop and went out back to clean them. He found an old brush and was able to remove most of the muck. Then he wiped them down with a soapy paper towel. He thought they looked presentable enough to be welcomed back into the house.

When his mom and Gracie came down for breakfast, Jem had already made the oatmeal and toast. He stopped short of making coffee for his mom because he didn't know how much of the grounds to use.

"Jem, what on earth?" his mother said, surprised by his gesture.

"You need a break, Mom."

"Well, that's the nicest thing someone's done for me for a long time. Thank you." She kissed him on the cheek.

"No big deal," he muttered to himself, thinking that his mom deserved good things to happen to her more frequently.

"So, Gracie, what do you think about being the angel this year?" he asked his sister.

"I get to stay up late," she said with pride. It would be the first time she would be up that late, and that made her feel like a big kid.

"You'll have to take a nap beforehand," Mrs. Jordan told her. She knew Gracie would fall asleep long before it was time for her to be out on Town Square at midnight to say her lines.

"Aww, no fair," Gracie responded.

"Don't worry. I'll make sure you're up in time. Jem, have you started your history project yet?" she asked, turning to her son.

"No. Marlee's sucked all the history out of the air, and there's none left for anybody else."

His mother laughed. "Whatever do you mean?" she asked.

"Marlee's been over at the library, looking into all that old archive stuff. She told me she was going to look for all the times the Christmas wish came true."

"Then you better get started, young man. I don't want to be the only parent who finds nothing on display at the library."

"I will, but I'm stuck. I don't know what to study yet," Jem told her.

That Monday, Jem returned to raking Mr. Trumbull's leaves. On Tuesday, he got caught. Mr. Trumbull didn't go all the way into town but doubled back after he rounded the corner. It seems he did notice that someone had been in his yard without his permission, and he was determined to find out who it was.

"You again!" Mr. Trumbull exclaimed as he snuck up on Jem.

Startled, Jem dropped the rake. "Mr. Trumbull, I thought you went into town."

"You think I didn't notice someone's been in my yard? Do you see that sign? It says, 'No Trespassing.' I don't like folks coming on my property for any reason. Now you get going, and don't come back!"

Jem was too scared to reply, so he grabbed his rake and ran. He couldn't hop on the bike fast enough. But the next day, he got his courage back, and he was waiting outside Mr. Trumbull's gate at three p.m.

"You again? I thought I told you to go away and leave me alone," Mr. Trumbull said.

"I know, sir, and I'm really sorry, but you didn't let me finish the job."

"Didn't let you finish!" Mr. Trumbull said in exasperation. "I didn't give you permission to start. You know what happens to people who keep bothering me and trespassing on my property?"

Jem didn't want to know and only said, "I'm not on your property right now. I'm on the sidewalk."

Mr. Trumbull said "humph" in about the same way Scrooge said "bah humbug."

"Please, Mr. Trumbull. I just want to show you I'm a good worker."

"You do, do you? And why would I want to know that? I suppose you think you can get on my good side, so I can let you traipse all over my house looking for the gold. Well, my answer is no. Now go away, and don't come back again."

When Jem heard him say something about gold, he forgot all about asking for chores.

"What gold? Do you have gold hidden in your house? I don't know anything about gold," Jem said.

He was so curious to find out what Mr. Trumbull meant that he thought his insides would burst.

"I said go away," Mr. Trumbull repeated.

"Why do people think you have gold in your house?"

"You hear me boy? I said go away and stop bothering me."

Jem was now starting to worry that his mission would fail, so he decided to forget about gold. In the short-term, earning some money from chores was more urgent.

"Please just let me finish raking. I promise I'm not here to look for gold. I don't know anything about your gold. I was hoping you might hire me to take care of your yard because your house is so run down, and your yard is a mess full of weeds and leaves. It really is a mess and needs a good tending to."

"What's your name, boy?"

"Jeremy, sir, but everyone calls me Jem. Jem Jordan."

"Well, Jeremy Jordan, I must say you show some gumption. Not many people do nowadays. You're the first person I haven't been able to scare away in I don't know how long. Come into the house. I guess I owe you that much for the work you've done."

Jem wasn't sure he wanted to go inside, not knowing what traps Mr. Trumbull might have set for people he caught "traipsing" in his house. He was hoping he could conduct business outside. But Jem desperately needed money, so he was willing to risk going inside the house. He said a quick prayer that he would come out alive.

While Mr. Trumbull was busy in the kitchen, fetching him some milk and cookies Jem had time to look around the room. He noticed all the decor was dark and dingy, and Jem thought it must be at least a hundred years old. It even looked more haunted inside than it did outside. There were cobwebs everywhere, and wallpaper was peeling off the walls in places. The carpets were worn, and everything looked dusty. It was like someone left and never came back, and now it was a hundred years later.

Jem heard Mr. Trumbull set the plates down on the dining room table. Mr. Trumbull called him to come and sit down.

"Now suppose you tell me the truth," Mr. Trumbull said.

"I did, sir," Jem tried to say between bites.

He didn't want to be impolite and talk with his mouth full, but Jem loved cookies and never passed them up. The milk was good, too, though it could have been a little colder.

"When I nearly ran you down, I was on my way to Mr. Bascombe's to see if I could do some work for him, and he said yes. So last Saturday, I went out there and worked all day, mending his fence, but I have to come back next Saturday to finish. He said he'd give me a hundred dollars but that means I only have two hundred, and the stove costs six hundred, so I'm a long way from being able to get one."

Jem stopped long enough to draw a breath, and Mr. Trumbull asked, "Why on earth do you need a stove?"

"Not me, sir. My mom. The festival is coming up, and that means my mom has to bake. She's about the best baker in the whole state, but our oven quit working, and if she can't bake, she won't get the money she makes from the festival. She works really hard but seems we can't make ends meet, so I'm trying to buy the stove for her in time for her to bake for the festival. Right now, she's using my friend, Marlee's, oven, but that's just until I can get us one of our own. I swear the money is not for me. It's for my mom. I'm a hard worker, sir. I just wanted to prove it to you by raking your yard. You got a pretty big yard, and there's a lot of leaves lying about."

"And so, you picked me out of all the other people in town because my house is run down, is that it?"

"Well, I don't want to be insulting, but it's a mess in that yard, Mr. Trumbull."

"And you are the man for the job. How old are you, Jeremy?"

"I'm thirteen, sir, but you can see how much work I've already done. I wanted to show you I can do it."

Mr. Trumbull sat deep in thought.

"Mr. Trumbull?" Jem said, not sure if the old man had fallen asleep.

"Yes?"

Jem wasn't sure how Mr. Trumbull would respond, but he let his curiosity get the better of him and asked him about the gold anyway.

"Aha! I thought so. All you people got some notion there's gold here. People come knocking day and night, digging in my yard. There is no gold here, and there has never been. Now you can finish up your cookies and get on out of here, and tell everyone else to stay away from me."

Now he'd gone and done it. Mr. Trumbull would never let him work now that he had made him suspicious of his motives.

He took a chance and asked, "Why on earth would anybody think you have gold here? I mean no disrespect, sir, but if I had gold, I'd fix my place up a little."

For the first time since 1987, when he had buried his wife, Mr. Trumbull laughed.

"You make a good point, young man. Maybe I can trust you after all. So, you don't know the story of the gold. Not sure whether that's good or bad. Good for me because the fewer people that know, the better. Bad for you because it doesn't seem they teach you young'uns much of the town's history anymore."

"Do you know a lot of history about this town? My history teacher is making us do a project for the festival, and I don't know what to do it on. It has to be something about this town."

"Well you do it on me, and maybe folks will get the word there isn't any gold out here. My great grandfather was Jedediah Smith's best friend. He was the only other person that knew where Smith found the gold. He was a Hiram as I am, and he arrived with his wife, my great grandmother Miriam, just after Smith did. At the time, Hiram didn't know anybody else was here. He built a cabin right here where the house now stands.

"One day, there was a terrible snowstorm, and Jedediah got caught in it. My great grandfather went out to the woodshed to bring in another load of wood for the fire when he saw a lump just lying there outside. It was Jedediah, and he was nearly dead. Miriam nursed him back to health, and if it wasn't for her quick thinking, Jedediah might have lost his hands and feet to frostbite. That's how they met. After that, Jedediah and my great grandfather hunted and fished together.

"Once people heard about the gold, they came flooding into town. No one found very much, and after a few years, they stopped looking, and many of them moved on. Well, my great grandfather was a smart man, and the people who searched for the gold went broke, but the people who opened businesses to serve the treasure hunters did well, and my great grandfather opened the Inn. It's the bed and breakfast they call it now. Some of those businesses are still here.

"Jedediah showed him where he found the gold and offered to let him have part of it, but Hiram said no, it was his fair and square, and he didn't want any part of it. He said he'd already seen too many men fall victim to riches and didn't want a thing more than to be able to take care of his family. There were nine children eventually."

"But why do people think there's gold here if your great grandfather didn't take any of it?"

"Because no one knows where Jedediah left it when he died. That is if he even had any to leave. Now that's enough for today. I've missed my trip to town, and folks will be speculating what happened to me. They'll probably take me for dead, so I'll leave them to their speculating when I show up on time tomorrow. Too tired to go now. You've gotten me out of my routine. Not sure that's all bad though. You come back in a day or two, and we'll see what needs to be done around here. In the meantime, get yourself over to that museum they call it, and see what you can find out about old Jedediah Smith and his gold. And you let me know if you find anything about the Trumbull family."

"I will, Mr. Trumbull. Thanks, sir. Thank you very much."

Jem left elated. Not only did he have the opportunity to make a little more money, now he knew what he would do for his history project.

CHAPTER 7

Liam and Patrick

Liam was opening another box of canned goods to put on the shelf at the H & M when his brother Patrick ran through the door.

"Liam, you've got to come home. They've taken Dad in an ambulance."

"What? What happened? Is he all right?"

"I don't know. Hurry!" Patrick urged him.

Just then, Mr. Caldwell came over to see what caused the commotion.

"Mr. Caldwell, I'm sorry, it's an emergency, and I have to go home," Liam said, clearly shaken by the news.

"Of course. Is everything all right?" Mr. Caldwell asked him.

"It's my dad. He's gone to the hospital. We don't know any more yet," Liam explained.

"Of course, go. Go! I'll finish up. Call and let me know how he is. Don't worry about coming in until you can," Mr. Caldwell said as Liam and Patrick took off running.

Liam was a good kid, Mr. Caldwell thought to himself as he watched them race down the street. He sure hoped everything was going to turn out all right with his father.

Liam had started working for him over the summer. It was only supposed to be a seasonal job. Liam was so dependable and such a good worker that when he asked if he could keep his job for a few hours during the week after school resumed, Mr. Caldwell was more than happy to say yes, as long as he had his parents' permission.

He, of course, knew the O'Brien family. Mr. O'Brien, Collin, came in from time to time, mostly for nails, small tools or plumbing supplies. Mrs. O'Brien came more frequently to purchase an item or two like milk or eggs. Most folks in Christmas got their groceries from the markets in Henderson. He couldn't compete with their prices, so he limited his inventory to what he knew they would need to replenish the most, like milk, bread, and eggs. It had been a good strategy as he had managed to stay in business. He knew his store wouldn't last much longer after he retired. Sooner or later, the bigger stores would swallow up his little one.

His two sons had grown up and moved away from Christmas. As sad as he was not to have them close by, he wanted them to have a brighter future. If they had stayed in town, they would have felt obligated to take over the store someday. He wanted more for them than that.

The store had given him a good living, though, he thought to himself. He had been able to put both boys through college and his oldest, Matt, had become an investment banker. His other son, Mark was a CPA. Both of them worked for large firms in Washington DC. He knew he made the right decision and was especially pleased that they lived close to each other. He and Patricia had often planned to move closer to them, especially once the grandchildren started arriving but since neither son had married, they still had time.

He went to pick up where Liam had left off and was finishing the task when another customer came in. He quickly threw the empty box into the back room and went up front to the register.

Liam and Patrick ran all the way home. There was a police car parked out front. Both boys were breathless and in a panic when they arrived. They burst through the front door.

"Mom! Mom!" they both cried in unison.

"It's okay. It's okay. Dad's pretty banged up, but he's going to be okay. At least, are you sure, Jefferson?" Liam could see the fear in his mother's eyes as she turned to address the sheriff.

Sheriff Jefferson Cooper was not only the town's sheriff, but he was also a close friend and attended church with the O'Briens.

"He hit some ice on the road and spun his truck into a tree, boys, but his injuries don't appear to be life-threatening. He was able to get out of the truck by himself. He has a pretty bad gash on his scalp, and his arm looks broken. You'll have to wait for the full report from the hospital to be sure. I'm going to take your mom there now," the sheriff told them.

"I'll call you as soon as I know something," their mother said as she grabbed her things and headed for the door. "I've already called your Aunt Jane, and she'll be here as fast as she can. I can't stop you from worrying, but please say your prayers for Dad."

Liam closed the door behind his mother and the sheriff.

"Liam?" Patrick looked like he was going to cry. Liam put his arm around his brother.

"I don't think the sheriff would tell us something that wasn't true. I know Dad must have hit his head hard, so he possibly has a concussion. And if he broke his arm, it'll just be in a cast for a month or two. I don't think they'll be home until tomorrow at the earliest. Do you have any homework you need help with?"

Liam knew it was best to keep his brother's mind off the situation and was glad when Patrick said he still hadn't figured out what to do for his history project.

"It's going to take a while for Aunt Jane to get here, and I doubt Mom will call until suppertime. We should have enough time to go over to the library. Maybe Miss Pemberton can give you an idea or two. She knows everything there is to know about this town. We'll leave a note for Aunt Jane, so she'll know where we are if she gets here before we get back."

Liam knew his dad wasn't out of the woods yet. They would do CT scans and x-rays to check the extent of the damage, and he silently prayed there would not be a significant head injury. The pickup was too old to have an airbag, but thankfully Dad always insisted they wear seatbelts.

They said a quick prayer together, and Liam wrote a note, which he taped to the fridge.

They found Miss Pemberton pushing the book cart down an aisle, placing books on their proper shelves. She turned when she heard their footsteps.

"Hello, boys. What brings you in today?" she asked them.

"Miss Pemberton, Patrick has to do a history project," Liam said to her.

"Oh yes, I know all about that. Mrs. Hudson's class."

"That's it," Patrick confirmed.

"Well, if you tell me what you want to research, I'll point you to the materials."

"That's just it, ma'am," Patrick said politely. "I don't know where to start or what to do. We thought maybe you could tell us something interesting about the town and then maybe I'd get an idea."

"I see. Well, come over here for a start." She led them over to the checkout desk, which was not a desk but a very long counter.

"Isn't this where you check out books?" Liam asked, not sure what she was trying to show them.

"I bet you didn't know that this counter was actually once a bar, and you're standing right now in what once was a saloon. And upstairs were the rooms that the barkeeper would rent out for twenty-five cents a night, or 'two bits' as they used to call it."

"Wow! Did anybody ever get killed, you know like they do in the movies when they find someone cheating at poker?" Patrick asked with great interest to hear more of the tale.

"Well, I'm not too sure about that," she smiled. "You'd have to look through all the old newspapers to see if there was any report of such a thing. We have lots of newspapers, but I haven't cataloged them in any way. If you're willing to look through them, you might find something," Miss Pemberton explained.

Patrick thought that sounded like a lot of work. He wasn't sure he was willing to invest that much time. If he didn't find anything, he'd be right back to where he was now and no closer to turning in a history project.

"Are there other buildings in town that used to be something else in the beginning? For example, what buildings are still here from when the town first started?" Patrick asked her.

"Come upstairs, and I'll introduce you to the plat records," Miss Pemberton said.

The what? Neither Liam nor Patrick knew what a plat record was, but they dutifully followed her up the old staircase.

Miss Pemberton thought Patrick was on to a good idea. She had wanted to research that very same topic herself but never found the time.

"Follow me over here, boys."

She led them to a room in the back that had shelves filled with old leather books. The books were large, about fifteen inches tall and bound in thick leather. They had raised ridges on the tops of the spines. No two of them matched except they were all a dark brown color, and they all smelled musty. On the bottom of each, there were identification numbers and what looked like date ranges had been written on the top between the two raised ridges.

Miss Pemberton pulled down the first book and told them it included the years from 1868 to 1874. She turned to the first page. The edges of the pages had darkened, and there were tears and worn spots from handling over the years. The handwriting had only faded a little, but it didn't look like modern-day handwriting so Patrick wasn't sure he would be able to read it.

"This is the first entry. See this number? That's what they call a plat number. Each piece of land was given a plat number. Here is a description of the property, how many acres, what the property was used for and the like. Commercial meant it was a business, agriculture meant it was a farm and so forth. This entry was marked agriculture, see?

"If this is checked, it indicated the property included water rights. That means whether there was a river or creek on the property. When neighbors feuded with each other, one neighbor might choose to dam up the stream on his land so the other neighbor couldn't get any water on his. Usually, neighboring properties both had water rights so they could prevent that sort of thing from happening.

"Now, this section recorded improvements, such as if a house, a building, or other structure was built on the property. Each documented improvement included the year it was finished.

"Over here," she said as she took them to another bookcase, "are all the recorded deeds by plat number. Each time a property sold to someone, the Town Clerk would find the plat number of the property and register the transfer. Now, if you knew the plat number to your house, you could look it up in this book and find out the history of when it was built. Then you could come over here to the deeds ledger and find out each year someone bought your house and who that was.

"That's as long as your house was built before the 1930s. That's when all the records were transferred to the county offices in Henderson. I either wasn't born or else I was a baby when that happened, but I remember my Papa said it was quite an undertaking. Since he was the bank president, they called on him if they needed to look at his mortgage records to clarify an entry in the deed ledger. He said it was quite a mess because the county wanted the records in a different order than Christmas kept them. They sent clerks out here, and all the records were rerecorded the way the county wanted them, by hand no less. But that was our lucky day because they left us these ledgers once they finished with them.

"Look, here's an example you might recognize. This plat number belongs to the Trumbull farm. I believe you know who Mr. Trumbull is. He lives on the edge of town."

"Yeah, that's the haunted house. Nobody goes by it. I bet if they ever tried to sell that place nobody would buy it," Patrick said.

He was finding this interesting, even though it sounded a little complicated following all the places Miss Pemberton showed them.

"Let's check to see if they ever did try to sell it. See here. This entry recorded it as a 123-acre-farm with one log cabin and one out-building. I think it says woodshed. There's an improvement recorded five years later. It says the cabin was torn down and replaced by a two-story house plus a cellar. There are no indications of further improvements, at least up until they transferred the records. If that is so, it means that the house today is original and was built in 1873.

"Look at this entry here. It shows that the land was subdivided. See these additional plat numbers? That means the original Mr. Trumbull sold some of his acres." She turned to the deed ledger.

"There are no entries here to show that the owners ever sold the house. That must mean that the Trumbull family have lived in it ever since it was built."

It was getting complicated, but Patrick got the gist of it, and he thought he'd be able to follow it without too much trouble. He knew Miss Pemberton would be able to help him if he got stuck.

"So, you mean I could start with the 1868 book, and it would show me the plat numbers that existed that year and those books over there with the deeds, would tell me who owned that property. Each year, I could see what was added to the town and who bought it. I could even find the plat number to this building, and the deed book would show me who built it and owned it over the years," Patrick said.

Miss Pemberton smiled and nodded. "Precisely. And also, what got taken away, don't forget, because a structure might be torn down or destroyed by fire. The book would show if that happened and whether they built something in its place."

"How would we be able to identify what plat number a particular place has? For example, how would we know what the plat number is for this building?" Liam asked.

"That is an excellent question, Liam. See those long skinny drawers over there?" Liam and Patrick looked where she was pointing. "Those are all the town maps. They aren't in any order, but you should find the year identified on them somewhere. There should be some survey maps that show the town divided by plat number. If you can't find it, you can go to the county offices in Henderson, and they'll give you one. Make sure you ask for the plat map for Christmas and not for the whole county," Miss Pemberton answered him.

"Thanks, Miss Pemberton. You have been a big help. I know what I'm going to do for my project now," Patrick said, relieved that he had finally settled on a topic.

"We have to go now. Patrick will be by as soon as he can. If you haven't heard yet, Dad was in an accident today, and they took him to the hospital," Liam told her as he turned back toward the stairs.

"Oh no! Is he going to be okay?" Miss Pemberton said, alarmed at the news.

"As far as we know, he has a gash on his scalp and a broken arm. We don't want to be too long because our Aunt Jane is coming, and Mom is supposed to call us with an update tonight," Liam informed her.

"Then you hurry along, and you let your family know I will keep you in my prayers."

"Thanks, Miss Pemberton, and thank you for your help," Patrick said.

By the time they got home, Aunt Jane still had not arrived. Both boys were hungry, so they fixed themselves an early dinner so Aunt Jane wouldn't need to cook for them.

As they sat down to eat, the phone rang, and Liam jumped up to answer it.

"Mom?" he said, with a catch in his voice.

"Dad is going to be fine. He has a nasty gash, which they stitched up right away, and he's also had a CT scan. There is no head injury thank the Lord. He's waiting to go down for an x-ray of his arm. The doctor doesn't know if he'll need surgery or not."

"Surgery?" Liam said. "What do you mean?"

"Don't worry. If it's a bad break, the doctors will operate to patch the bone with a metal plate. If the break is simple, they'll just set it and put a cast on. We won't be home tonight, though."

"Okay, I understand. I'll tell Aunt Jane when she gets here," Liam said.

"You mean she's not there yet?" his mother asked.

"Hold on. I think that's Aunt Jane now," Liam said just as the door opened.

"Is that Molly?" Aunt Jane asked as she walked through the door breathlessly. She saw the phone in Liam's hand. "Let me talk to her, please."

Liam handed the phone to his aunt. The two sisters talked briefly, and Aunt Jane received instructions for taking care of the household. "Don't worry about anything here, Molly. Just get Collin better. Call me back when you know about his arm," she told her sister as she hung up.

When it was time for the boys to turn in, Aunt Jane assured them she would wake them if there were any news. Patrick fell asleep right away, but Liam tossed and turned for a while. He was relieved that his father's injuries were not worse than they were, but he thought of a major problem no one had mentioned yet.

How on earth was his dad going to find the money to replace the pickup?

CHAPTER 8

Emergency

Jem returned to Mr. Trumbull's the following day. He met Mr. Trumbull as he was coming back from his trip to town, having taken to heart Mr. Trumbull's comment that Jem had interrupted his routine.

"I almost thought you weren't coming back," Mr. Trumbull greeted him.

"No, sir, I gave you my word. I just didn't want to break your routine again," Jem replied.

"There was quite a hubbub when I didn't show up yesterday. I think we gave those busybodies in town quite a scare. Well, I'm happy to know they either missed me or they have nothing else to talk about in town. Come inside. I still have some cookies left. And see here, I've bought some new ones, chocolate chip. You like them I hope?"

"They're the best, Mr. Trumbull."

They made their way inside, and once again Jem looked around the place while Mr. Trumbull fussed in the kitchen.

"Can I help you, Mr. Trumbull?" Jem asked as he entered the kitchen.

"Yes, I think I will take you up on your offer. My trip into town seems to have worn me out more than usual. Fetch the milk from the refrigerator over there, please, and then see if you can reach a plate from that cabinet."

"Wow, Mr. Trumbull. I think your stove is older than ours!" Jem exclaimed as he opened the cabinet just to the left of it. After getting a plate down, he retrieved the milk from the fridge.

"You know, Mr. Trumbull, I appreciate your hospitality, but you don't have to serve me milk and cookies every time I come."

"Balderdash. We have negotiations to tend to. Haven't you heard that if I ply you with cookies and milk, I will have the upper hand in the negotiations and get the better deal?"

Jem wasn't quite sure he understood the point Mr. Trumbull was making. "Mr. Trumbull, I'm just a kid, but I'll give you a good deal with or without the cookies."

Mr. Trumbull laughed. "Young Jeremy, you are a man of integrity. I like that. Now let's sit down, and you tell me how much your raking job is worth."

"I don't want anything for what I've already done. I was making an investment so to say, to prove that I can do a good job," Jem told him.

"Well, we'll see. Suppose you tell me something about yourself. I like to know about a person before I hire him."

Jem wasn't sure just what Mr. Trumbull wanted to know about a thirteen-year-old. Jem didn't exactly have a resume.

"I live with my mom and sister, Gracie. She's nine," he started. "We live on the other side of Town Square. My mom works for Dr. Millman. I go to middle school. That's why I was curious about the gold because I have to do a history project about this town."

"What of your father?" Mr. Trumbull asked.

"I don't have a father. At least, I did have one, but he left us when Gracie was a baby."

"What do you mean he left you?" Mr. Trumbull asked.

"Well, he just went out one night and never came back. We haven't seen or heard from him since," Jem explained.

"You mean your father brought you and your sister into the world and then shirked his responsibility for you?" Mr. Trumbull said, appalled that such a thing was possible.

"I guess so if you put it that way," Jem responded.

"Humph. Never heard of such atrocious behavior. Never mind. You've turned into a very fine young man. I am sure your mother is very proud of you," Mr. Trumbull said.

"Thank you, sir. But I wouldn't mind if you reminded her of that from time to time. She says I'm incorrigible. I'm not sure what that means, but I don't think she's proud of it."

Mr. Trumbull laughed again and wondered why he hadn't found more to laugh at all these years. For many years, he convinced himself he disliked children. Perhaps if he'd met more like young Jeremy, he'd have changed his mind a lot sooner. Mr. Trumbull found he looked forward to his near-daily meetings with this young man.

"What do you like most about school?" Mr. Trumbull asked as Jem took a sip of milk.

"Well, it's not history," Jem quipped.

Mr. Trumbull laughed again. Jem had a way of expressing himself that reminded him of his favorite TV comedian, Jack Benny.

"History's not that bad. You live as long as I have and you've lived through a lot of it," Mr. Trumbull told him.

"Yeah, I guess that's true enough. I really don't like any subject enough to get excited about it. Now you take my friend Patrick, Patrick O'Brien. He loves math and science but me, I'm just your average student."

"You said you had some work to do out at Bascombe's," Mr. Trumbull inquired.

"I have to finish repairing his fence. It's a pretty big one. I've been replacing broken rails, about a hundred of them. I hope to be finished this coming Saturday. Mr. Trumbull, why do you keep it so dark in here?" Jem asked, abruptly changing the subject.

"Can't see any use in drawing the curtains only to have to close them up again. I don't spend much time in these rooms," Mr. Trumbull replied.

"Maybe you should just take them down. It sure would be a lot cheerier in here," Jem suggested.

"Never mind about my curtains. What work do you think you can do for me?" Now it was Mr. Trumbull's turn to change the subject.

"Well, your yard is a mess. I need to complete the raking I started, but then I could clean out your flowerbeds. They're pretty choked with weeds, and they need mulching after that. I'd be willing to paint your house except I'm sure my mom wouldn't let me go that high on a ladder. You have any junk in the attic you want to have hauled away?" Jem said, listing off what chores he could think of.

"How much is it worth to you to bring my rose gardens back to life?" Mr. Trumbull asked.

"I will do the weeding and mulching now and come back in the spring to feed and trim them for fifty dollars, and you purchase the mulch."

"How do I know you'll come back in the spring?" Mr. Trumbull said, sounding like he wasn't sure he could trust a thirteen-year-old to remember a promise.

"Because you said I'm a man of integrity. I give you my word," Jem replied

"And when will you start?" Mr. Trumbull asked.

"I'll come back a week from Saturday. If you order the mulch on Monday, Mr. Caldwell can bring it out by the end of the week," Jem promised.

"All right, we have a deal. You finish cleaning up my yard then we'll see about my attic. Now, Jeremy, as much as I like your company, I'm afraid I'm going to have to ask you to finish your milk and cookies. I feel quite tired and will head upstairs for a nap," Mr. Trumbull said.

"Okay, Mr. Trumbull. I can't thank you enough. I'll do a great job for you, sir."

Jem thought Mr. Trumbull did look pretty worn out. *Guess it's not easy being old,* he thought. Jem had never met anyone as old as Mr. Trumbull.

That Saturday, Jem worked straight through the day and as far into the evening as he could still see and managed to finish Mr. Bascombe's fence. Mr. Bascombe had even given him a ten-dollar tip. Mr. Bascombe said to treat himself to ice cream with it since he had worked so hard.

"Please call me if there's anything else you want me to do," Jem said as he handed Mr. Bascombe his phone number. "I'll be back after Thanksgiving to start practicing for Nativity Night."

Tuesday evening, Jem had to run down to the H & M to pick up something for his mother. While he was looking for it on the shelves, he overheard two women mention Mr. Trumbull by name.

"When Trumbull missed that day a week or so back, we all thought something happened to him, but then he showed up next day right as rain. Now he's up and missed two straight days," said one of the ladies.

"You know that old coot has no one out there with him. If he died in that house, who would miss him? Two days you say. Maybe someone ought to have Sheriff Cooper go out and check on him. It's not like Trumbull to miss two days," the other lady added.

When Jem heard this conversation, he forgot all about what brought him into the H & M. He hurriedly found Mr. Caldwell.

"Mr. Caldwell, did Mr. Trumbull order mulch from you yesterday?" Jem asked him.

"Mulch, why ever would he need mulch?" Mr. Caldwell queried.

"I'm doing some yard work for him. He said he would order the mulch," Jem explained.

"I've not seen him yesterday nor today."

"I'm going out to check on him. I think something's wrong."

With that Jem ran through the door and hopped on the bike. He was worried and hoped everything was okay. He sure hoped Mr. Trumbull had an explanation. Maybe he just forgot.

He got to the house in record time but out of breath. He rang the doorbell twice and pounded on it loudly while calling "Mr. Trumbull, Mr. Trumbull, it's Jem, are you all right?"

He didn't get an answer, so he started peering through the windows. It was too dark to see anything. He tried banging on the door again, louder this time, but still got no response. He tried to open the door but found it was locked. He ran around back, but the back door was locked, too. He then decided to check each window to see if by any chance one had been left unlatched. On his fifth try, he found a kitchen window that he could raise slightly. He pushed and pushed, but it only moved a crack.

He needed to stand on something to get better leverage. He found a couple of old wooden crates. After mustering all his strength, he finally raised the window enough that he could shimmy through the opening. Once he was inside, he shouted again, but again got no response. Really worried, he raced from room to room but didn't find Mr. Trumbull.

At the bottom of the stairs, he called again. "Mr. Trumbull, it's Jem, Jeremy, are you all right?" When he was greeted with nothing but silence, he called out, "I'm coming upstairs."

He thought he heard a noise but couldn't tell where it was coming from, so he had to run from room to room once again. Finally, he opened a bedroom door and saw a figure lying in bed.

"Mr. Trumbull? It's Jeremy. Are you all right?"

Mr. Trumbull seemed to be sleeping, so Jem reached out to touch his forehead. Mr. Trumbull opened his eyes slightly and said, "Who is it?"

"It's Jeremy, sir. I got worried when they said you hadn't been to town, and you didn't order the mulch. Are you feeling all right?"

"Jem. Jem, is it? I had a boy once. Where is he? Go ask my wife. Send him to me." Mr. Trumbull was mumbling and could barely be heard.

Jem wasn't sure he caught all the words correctly, but he thought Mr. Trumbull was asking for his wife. This worried him.

"Mr. Trumbull, what are you talking about?"

Mr. Trumbull could only mutter, and he appeared to be drifting off again. Jem decided he had better call the sheriff, remembering the conversation he overheard at the H & M.

"Mr. Trumbull, do you have a phone?"

He got no response and didn't want to wait for one. He looked around the room but didn't see a phone. If anything, it was darker up here than it was downstairs. He decided to look in the kitchen. Most people had a phone in their kitchens.

After racing downstairs, he didn't find one there either. *Maybe in the front room*, he thought. He actually found the phone in the hallway. It was an old rotary phone.

"What kind of phone is this?" he said out loud. After several tries, he figured out how to dial 911 by putting his finger into the hole by the first number and turning it clockwise. When he let go, the dial spun back to its original position. He had to wait for this to finish before he could dial the next number. *Boy, this is taking forever*, he thought, frustrated and worried. *Thank goodness phones don't work like this anymore.*

When dispatch answered, Jem told the lady to send the sheriff out to Mr. Trumbull's right away. Jem unlocked the front door and left it open a crack. He ran upstairs quickly, but there was no change in Mr. Trumbull. He still appeared to be sleeping.

After what seemed to be an eternity, Jem finally heard a car pull up, and shortly after that, an ambulance siren. It turned out that the sheriff had heard Mr. Trumbull had not been to town for two days, and when dispatch told him some kid called and said to get out to Trumbull's place, he alerted the paramedics to be on the safe side.

"Jem, what on earth are you doing here?" the sheriff asked him.

"I think Mr. Trumbull's sick. He was talking funny, and now he just seems like he's sleeping and won't wake up."

The paramedics entered the front door. "Take us to him," they directed.

Jem climbed the stairs quickly and led them to Mr. Trumbull's room. The paramedics took over, so the sheriff pulled Jem out into the hallway. One of the paramedics found them in the hall and asked if Mr. Trumbull had any next of kin.

"There's no one else here, and his wife died away back. He might have a son, he talked about a son, but he was talking funny, so I don't know. There's no one I know of," Jem answered.

"What do you have?" the sheriff asked the paramedic, in a low voice in case it was bad news.

"He needs to be transported. His blood pressure is dangerously low, and he's incoherent. We need to get him to the hospital right away, but we need his authorization," the paramedic told him.

Jem overheard them and said, "Let me try." He entered the room and knelt by Mr. Trumbull.

"Mr. Trumbull, can you hear me?" Jem said, trying to rouse the old man.

"Is that Jeremy?" Mr. Trumbull said in a weak voice.

"Yes, sir, it's me. Mr. Trumbull, you're sick. The paramedics are here to take you to the hospital. They've come to help you. Is it okay if they take you?"

"Jeremy? I feel poorly," Mr. Trumbull managed to say.

"I know, sir. I brought some people to help you. Can they take you to the hospital? Please, sir, you're very sick, and I'm getting worried about you." Jem started to cry, a tear escaping down his cheek.

Mr. Trumbull didn't say anything for a long time, and Jeremy was worried. After a long pause, he finally said, "Jeremy. Good boy. Don't cry, lad,"

"Oh, Mr. Trumbull, will you let them take you? To the hospital? Please, sir."

"Good lad, you take me to the hospital." Mr. Trumbull closed his eyes, his energy gone.

That was enough for the paramedics to start moving. They got him on the gurney and into the back of the ambulance, and Jem waited to see them leave, sirens wailing.

He didn't know if he was going to be in trouble with the sheriff. After all, he had come in through the window. The window! He had better go into the kitchen to close it.

"Do you want to explain how you knew to come out here?"

Jem was sure he was going to be in trouble now. He had closed the window but left it unlatched as a precaution in case he had to get in again someday. The sheriff was waiting for him by the front door.

"I've been coming out here to do some yard work, and Mr. Trumbull was supposed to order mulch for me yesterday. I happened to be in the H & M to pick up something for my mother. Oh boy, she's going to wonder what happened to me.

"Two ladies were talking and said Mr. Trumbull had missed coming into town two days in a row, so I asked Mr. Caldwell. He said no, Mr. Trumbull had not ordered the mulch, so I knew something was up. I couldn't get in 'til I found a window I could shimmy through."

"You did the right thing, Jem, and I'm proud of you for being responsible. But you should have called me first. I have to hand it to you, though. Most kids wouldn't come near this place."

"Is he dying?" Jem asked the sheriff, worried about Mr. Trumbull.

"I don't know, Jem," the sheriff said compassionately. He could see how worried Jem was. "They'll do everything they can for him. But you know he's ninety-two, and that's a long life. Say your prayers, and I will, too. We're all in God's hands no matter what age we are."

Jem rode back home and almost forgot to pick up what his mom wanted at the H & M. He barely knew Mr. Trumbull, but he had started to think of him as a friend. Now it appeared he wouldn't be doing any work for him and he wondered what to do about that. Of course, he had his history project to work on and maybe he shouldn't put that off any longer.

The sheriff had promised to call him if any word came in about Mr. Trumbull's condition.

I guess I have a free Saturday now. Phooey, Jem thought. Working in Mr. Trumbull's yard would have been so much better than spending Saturday with a bunch of old papers. Jem knew he had no more excuses and had better get started. His history project wouldn't write itself.

CHAPTER 9

The Last Will
and Testament of
Jedediah Smith

Marlee, too, realized she couldn't put her project off any longer, so Saturday after lunch, she went to the library. She hoped Miss Pemberton could help her get started. Marlee had been coming in for several Saturdays to browse but hadn't found anything useful. She realized she was just making excuses and deliberately procrastinating.

The sign at the checkout counter said Miss Pemberton was upstairs, so Marlee climbed the old staircase and found her wiping down a display case toward the front of the building.

"I just had some visitors, and the little boy left his sticky finger-prints on the glass. Not that I mind, I love curious children, and I am always glad to show off our historical artifacts. Whatever brings you in, oh, the history project again. What are you researching?"

"You know I'm Mary this year. And you know the legend—"

"Of the Christmas wish, for who holds the Baby Jesus figure," Miss Pemberton said, finishing Marlee's sentence.

"I know everyone thinks I'm being superstitious," Marlee said, "but I thought, if there is any truth to it, I might find records of past wishes that came true. Oh, I know it sounds silly when I say it out loud. I also want to research the figure itself, where it came from, how old it is, whatever I can find out about it in case I don't find much about the legend. I'm sure you think I'm crazy."

"Well, not really, Marlee. If there were any interesting stories, I am sure they would have been reported. Why don't we begin with learning about Jedediah Smith? After all, he is the one who brought the figure here from Italy."

Miss Pemberton took Marlee over to a tall display case with several shelves of artifacts on them.

"What do you see?" Miss Pemberton asked her.

"There's some old eyeglasses, an old ink pen, and a Bible, and I guess that must be some kind of wallet," Marlee responded.

"That's a man's purse. Men carried purses in that day, though of course, they didn't look like the kind we women carry. That's what he used to hold his money and important papers."

"And there's an old hat, and some kind of canvas bag like the postman carries who delivers the mail," Marlee continued, listing additional items in the case.

"Jedediah Smith didn't own much more than these items when he died. That's not much for a man who was supposed to have owned a fortune in gold," Miss Pemberton stated.

"I see he owned a Bible, and it looks very well used. Was he really a believer?" Marlee asked her.

"Oh yes, indeed he was. You know he started the town of Christmas to honor the Advent. After he returned from Italy with the Baby Jesus figure, the same one we use today, he started the manger scene we now call Nativity Night. He wanted the whole town to know why Jesus was born. I presume there were a lot of lawless men back in his day when gold fever was at its pitch."

"Did he live here in town? I never heard any house around here being his," Marlee asked.

"Oh no, he lived up in the mountains, in the same log cabin he built when he first arrived. He refused to move to town as he preferred his humble dwelling. He said he felt closer to his maker when he was in the elements. He was a frugal and a very humble man."

"Is his cabin still there? I never heard anyone talk about it, either," Marlee asked, thinking how she would love to see where he once lived.

"I cannot say for sure, as it's been over a century since he lived there. I know there are treasure hunters who come from time to time trying to find gold up there. I rather imagine they have torn the place to pieces looking for it. We should have raised the money a long time ago to preserve that place. I saw it when I was a girl. It was mostly intact back then, but that was a long, long time ago," Miss Pemberton told her, trying to remember just how long ago it had been.

"Why do people look for gold after all this time? I thought the gold rush ended when no one else found gold. Why would anyone keep looking a hundred and fifty years later?" Marlee asked her.

"You are right of course, Marlee, but there is no stopping gold fever once a person gets it. It's like playing the mega millions lottery. The bigger the pot, the more people buy tickets. Since they have a winner from time to time, people think there's a reason to buy a ticket. So, people keep looking for the spot where Jedediah found his gold. Their chances probably aren't any better than the lottery, but that doesn't stop them. But there is another reason. Come over here," Miss Pemberton said, leading Marlee over to another display.

"Folks are also looking for the gold Jedediah supposedly hid. There has never been a report of anyone finding it, so as far as anyone knows, it's still hidden, waiting for the Lord to lead someone to it."

"The Lord? What do you mean? What does the Lord have to do with it?" Marlee said. "Why would someone think God would help them find gold that had been hidden for over a hundred years or longer?"

"Read the will. This is Jedediah's last will and testament." Miss Pemberton showed Marlee the display case hanging on the wall that had a piece of yellowed and cracked paper inside. The writing was hard to read, not because it was faded, but because it was in an unfamiliar script. No one had handwriting like that nowadays. There was a printed copy of the will on the wall next to it. Miss Pemberton knew most people would prefer to read the card instead. It read:

> I am a miracle of Christmas. I was left on the doorsteps of a small church on the day of my birth, 25 December 1829. The pastor and his wife were elderly, but being childless, they raised me as their own. By the time I was twelve, they were both gone, but they left me their legacy of love, and they taught me about the real meaning of Christmas. I wandered for many years, scraping by a living, doing many bad things to stay alive. But in 1865, when Mr. Lincoln was felled by an assassin's bullet, I found my Savior Jesus. That is also the year I found gold in the hills above this town. So, I started the town of Christmas, and I asked everyone who came to join me in a public celebration. We have done it ever since. Since I never married and am childless and being there's no other family I could ever find, I leave behind the rest of my gold to my town. I figure the Lord will let you know where it is in his time. In the meantime, it is my prayer that this town of Christmas will never forget the true meaning of its name. Celebrate Christmas every day, and if you love him, continue the town's celebration, which we established in 1868 and have done ever since. It is now getting close to my time. I, Jedediah Christmas Smith, write this in my own hand and this constitutes my last will and testament. I have nothing to leave behind except the gold, and I hope and pray, my legacy of celebrating Christmas.
>
> Signed by me, Jedediah Christmas Smith, 19 July 1910

"So, you see, he says he left behind his gold. He left nothing that said where, however, and there has never been a report that it was found. Possibly someone did and just took off with it without saying anything. There was no government back then that came breathing down your neck. Not like today," Miss Pemberton concluded.

Just then Jem came upstairs.

"Oh, it's Jem! I wonder what brings you here," Marlee laughed.

"Yeah, I know, and Patrick's on his way up, too," Jem replied.

"Well, you will have plenty of records to sort through and share," Miss Pemberton said as Patrick came to the top of the stairs.

"If the three of you will come over here, let's see. Patrick, do you know what ledgers you are using?" Miss Pemberton asked him.

"Yes, Miss Pemberton, the ones you showed me the other day," he answered her.

"How's your father by the way?" she asked him.

"He's fine. He has a cast on his arm, and his stitches are coming out at the end of the week, but he's been able to go back to work," Patrick told her.

"I am so happy to hear that. You give him my best," Miss Pemberton said, happy that Mr. O'Brien hadn't done worse damage to himself.

"I will, Miss Pemberton. I can get started on my own." Patrick left them for the room where the plat and deed ledgers were kept.

"What's Patrick doing? Do you know Miss Pemberton?" Jem asked hoping it wasn't the same thing he wanted to do.

"Yes, I believe he is going to search all the land records so he can describe what made up the town in the beginning. Now, Marlee, you will need to use these papers and clippings over here for your Christmas wish research. There are several boxes here, and that leaves you, Jem. What is your topic?"

"I want to know about the gold!" Jem answered enthusiastically.

"Well, if you are talking about where to find it, I'm afraid your project is going to be short. We do have some information here that you're welcome to sort through. I am sure you will find plenty on what the town was like during and after our gold rush," Miss Pemberton said as she showed him a shelf of boxes.

"Do you know if there's anything on the Trumbull family? Hiram Trumbull was Jedediah Smith's best friend, and lots of people have been pestering the current Mr. Trumbull to look for gold on his property," Jem asked her.

"So, you've heard that story too. In that case, I would recommend you look through the same batch of records that Marlee is using. Maybe you can help each other out if you each take a box and tell the other if you find anything of interest," Miss Pemberton suggested.

"That's a good idea!" Jem said, eager to try this approach because he thought it might cut his effort in half.

Marlee, however, was not sure she wanted any assistance. Jem might overlook something critical, and she didn't want to rely on him. Marlee preferred to study the documents by herself, even if it took longer. However, she didn't say this to Jem.

"Now, Marlee, I have additional materials regarding the festival that are over here in these books. I'm afraid both of you are probably going to find it hit-or-miss as there is no order to any of these records," Miss Pemberton said as she pointed out the books.

Leave it to Patrick the brain to pick an approach that was straightforward and logical. No hit-or-miss for him, Marlee thought to herself. She could see he was already pouring over some large books and was steadily writing notes.

"I do have a ledger here that lists all of the cast members of Nativity Night by year. I think if you look through it, you will find your dad was once a king," Miss Pemberton said.

"If I was going to try to find Smith's cabin, Miss Pemberton, where would I look?" Marlee asked her.

"Oh my, that is a tall order. I know you start at the back of the church and go straight up the mountain. Wait a minute. Patrick is researching the land records. He's looking for a map with the plat numbers assigned. With that, he can find who owned what piece of property," Miss Pemberton responded.

"The what numbers?" Marlee asked.

"Plat numbers. Every parcel of land was assigned a plat number, and every plat number was owned by someone. If you can find that

Jedediah Smith's property was given a plat number, you could find it on the map. Patrick is researching that, so you'll have to ask him if he has found a plat map yet. If not, all I can say is you go straight up the mountain, but I don't think there are any trails left after all this time. I only found it by chance. You know, that's what got me interested in history, standing in the very place where Jedediah Smith lived and touching the same things he touched. I could almost feel his presence."

I wish you could feel his gold, Jem thought to himself.

"So, if there's anything about the Christmas wish legend, it would be in the newspaper accounts," Marlee stated. Miss Pemberton nodded her head.

Now that the conversation had turned to Christmas wishes Jem was ready to get started on his box of records. He, too, was interested in finding Smith's cabin. He'd ask Marlee if she intended to try and find it. He wanted to go with her. But for right now, he needed to find out what was reported about Smith's gold discovery and the ensuing gold rush that brought hundreds of men to this area.

"I'll tell you one story of a wish that came true," Miss Pemberton said as Marlee set a box down on the table.

"What is it, Miss Pemberton?" Marlee said.

"When I was Mary, my wish was that my school teacher would get married and move away. Now I know that violated the so-called rules, I wasn't supposed to ask for something for myself, but I didn't believe in the legend anyway. I only wished it because I didn't like her, and she was really and truly a mean old lady. I shouldn't be talking about her like that, but believe me, she was mean. And lo and behold, the next year she got married and moved away, and no one even knew she was courting! But afterward, I felt guilty that I wished it. Funny, I still think about her to this day. I hope she met Jesus along the way. I'm sure she can't still be alive after all this time. Just goes to show you. Use your wish well, Marlee."

With that, Miss Pemberton went back to her library duties and left the three of them to study for their projects.

"Are you going to try to find Smith's cabin?" Jem asked Marlee. "I want to go with you if you do."

"Let's ask Patrick if he's found a whatever it's called number for it." They interrupted Patrick to ask the question, but he said no, he had not found any reference to Jedediah Smith's cabin. So far, it appeared it was not considered part of the town for which they kept records, but he said he would let them know if he ran across something.

After a couple of hours of reading ancient newspaper accounts, Marlee learned more than she really wanted to know about the Christmas festival. She'd found descriptions of the early years when all they did was put up a tree decorated with homemade ornaments and present the live manger scene. They didn't include any live animals back then since most people owned livestock and didn't need to see what a sheep or donkey looked like. They sang Christmas carols, and someone read the Christmas story from the book of Luke. Smith insisted on having the manger scene every year in Town Square.

Boy, they really made a big deal out of this Christmas thing. Marlee enjoyed celebrating Christmas as much as the next person, but she didn't see why you needed to follow a tradition year after year. Though it was interesting that all these years they had used the same Baby Jesus figure and she would get to hold it, holding 150 years of history in her arms. And who knows what history it had before then? That is what she was hoping to find, too.

She did find the article from the time Smith returned to Christmas from Rome where he had purchased it. He bought it from a bazaar, and the vendor told him it was three hundred years old. The report didn't reveal much more information except that it might have come from a Catholic Church or Monastery.

She found a few stories of wishes. In 1882, it was reported that there was a terrible flu outbreak and several children were near death at Christmastime. Not a single one died. Marlee thought maybe that was a miracle because the flu generally killed a lot of people back then.

There was another report of a family by the name of Compton on the verge of losing their farm. Mr. Compton found three half buried gold coins in his back garden and was sure they had not been there before. Of course, there had been a heavy rainfall the night before, which could have washed away the soil and exposed them. Marlee thought that sounded more like Jedediah Smith coming to the rescue.

There were more accounts of illnesses being survived and financial disasters being averted, but Marlee could find no consistent evidence that proved they were not just coincidences. Then an article caught her eye, "Boy Miraculously Healed by Christmas Festival Wish," and it started out by saying, "Eight-year-old Christmas resident walks again after a three-month illness that left him paralyzed." The article was dated 1911, which happened to be the year after Smith died. Apparently, they thought the child had the flu, but his illness worsened until he could barely breathe, and they thought he was in a coma. None of the doctors treating him believed the child would live. His mother refused to leave him in the hospital for fear she would not be there if he should worsen. It didn't appear the doctors could do much for him, anyway.

The worst part of the illness lasted a few weeks. When it appeared the boy would live, his mother discovered he could no longer use his legs. The doctor was called immediately but had no diagnosis or cure. The article ended by saying, "Today young Master Taylor is an active eight-year-old playing with his friends and running in the fields." Asked what residents of Christmas thought about this development, most attributed his healing to the collective prayers of the whole town, a mother's tender care, and the mercies of God. But one little girl by the name of Rebecca Trumbull said, "'I knew all along he was going to be healed. That was my Christmas wish. I got to be Mary and hold the Christ Child last Christmas.' Make of it what you will, one family in Christmas is celebrating Christmas every day this year."

Marlee looked again at the girl's name. She had to be part of the Trumbull family whose house was the haunted one on the way to Bascombe's farm.

"Hey, Jem," she called out to him. "Don't you know, Mr. Trumbull? I heard them say you were out at his place and had to call an ambulance."

"Yeah, I know him. He's in the hospital right now. They said it was pneumonia. Why?" Jem left his seat and came over to see what Marlee had found.

"There's an article here about a Rebecca Trumbull. How old is Mr. Trumbull now?"

"I think he's ninety-two," Jem told her.

"So that would make him born in 1926 or thereabouts. This article is dated 1911, so Rebecca would have been born in 1898, give or take a year if she was thirteen when she was Mary. That would mean she'd have to be an aunt, not a sister. Are you going into Henderson anytime soon? If so, are you going to stop and see him?" Marlee asked Jem.

"I asked my mom to take me, but she's not sure when we can go," Jem responded.

"Can you ask him to tell you about Rebecca? See if he knows anything about her Christmas wish." She hoped Jem wouldn't forget to ask Mr. Trumbull. It would be interesting to find out if he knew of any Trumbull family lore regarding the wish.

"Sure, I'll ask him." Just then, Jem remembered that Mr. Trumbull asked him for anything he found out about his family.

"Can you get Miss Pemberton to make a copy of that story? If I take it to him, maybe he'll remember her better," he said.

Marlee looked at the clock and realized she had to get home. She was disappointed that she didn't feel any closer to her goal than when she started. Maybe Patrick had the better of the projects.

"I've got to get going, Jem. I'll ask Miss Pemberton to have a copy of this downstairs for you when you leave. Patrick, I have to go. Good luck on your research," she called out to Patrick.

"Okay, Marlee. See you later," Patrick responded.

When Marlee got home, she found her mother on the phone. Her voice quieted as soon as Marlee entered the room. That meant her mother was talking about something she didn't want her to hear. Marlee fixed a snack and tried not to eavesdrop, but she couldn't help but hear her mother say, "However will they manage the medical bills, not to mention the loss of the truck?" and knew she was talking about the O'Briens.

She didn't hear the person on the other end say, "Well, Jenna Lee, I guess they'll manage as well as we all do."

"I know, but it's Christmastime," her mother said before hanging up.

Maybe that's my Christmas wish, Marlee thought.

CHAPTER 10

Marlee's Trial

No one knew Marlee's mother was expecting, not even her mother, but she lost her baby that following week.

Parker had come to Marlee's school to get her, so they had called her out of class. She nearly had a heart attack when she saw Park out front waiting to take her home and was sure someone in her family had died.

"What is it? Tell me. Is it Grams?" she asked him frantically.

"No, it's Mom, not Grams. All I know is she called Dr. Millman, and when he got there, he called an ambulance."

"But what's wrong with her? She's never been sick."

"I don't know any more than that. We'll just have to wait until we get home. Mom called Grams to come over."

Their grandmother was standing in the doorway when they arrived.

"Oh, Grams, what is wrong? What did Dr. Millman say?" Marlee asked.

"I don't know yet. She was having some sort of abdominal pain. Your Aunt Emma Lee is going to meet her at the hospital, and she'll call us as soon as she can," her grandmother replied.

"What about Dad, does he know?" Park asked.

"I talked with your father about an hour ago. He's driving straight through, but the earliest he can get to the hospital is about three in the morning."

"What can we do, anything?" Park asked.

"Just say your prayers. When we know what's going on, we'll figure out what comes next. No need to put the cart before the horse. Now you best get your schoolwork done, and I'll go clean the kitchen and see what I can make for dinner."

Marlee had her notes for the history project, but she was so worried about her mother that she made a mess of trying to organize them, so she abandoned the effort. She decided to do her math homework instead. It was easier to work one calculation at a time. Math was so much more straightforward than history.

Park was just as distracted from his schoolwork, so he turned his music up high to take his mind off of his worries.

Marlee ended up taking a nap, something she never did unless she was sick. She woke up when she heard the phone ringing. She rushed down the stairs in case that was her aunt calling.

"I see. Give Jenna Lee our love and tell her Trent is on his way and will get there around two or three in the morning. Love you." With that, Grams hung up the phone. When she turned, she saw Marlee standing there.

"Go get your brother."

Grams looked like it was terrible news, and Marlee was nearly in a panic when she knocked on Parker's door. He had the music turned up so loud she had to bang. Not only had he not heard the phone ring, he couldn't even hear her knocking. She pounded the door again.

When he finally opened the door, she said, "Park, why do you have it turned up so loud? Grams wants us downstairs. She just got off the phone with Aunt Emma Lee."

Parker turned off the radio and closed his door behind him. It was a somber group that met their grandmother in the kitchen.

"Your mom is going to be all right," Grams told them.

"What's the matter with her?" Marlee asked.

"I'm sorry to have to tell you she miscarried. She was about four months along."

"Mom was pregnant? She never said," Park remarked, surprised that his parents would keep that kind of news from them that long.

"She didn't know herself. Sometimes, you think it's something else going on."

"I know about the change, Grams. I believe it is not infrequent that women find themselves 'with child' when they believe they are no longer able to conceive," Parker said.

Park reads too much, Marlee thought to herself.

"Oh, I think she's still too young for that," Grams said. "She has to stay a night or two in the hospital. They gave her a blood transfusion, so the doctor wants to make sure she doesn't need another one before sending her home. Then she must be on bed rest for a week or two."

"Did Aunt Emma Lee say if it was a boy or girl?" Marlee almost whispered. She was trying to get over the shock of what she was just told.

"I'm sorry, Marlee, it was a girl." Grams knew how much Marlee had wished for a sister, even though she hadn't said anything about it for some time.

"I'm going to Miss Belle's." Marlee stood up to go.

"It's almost time for supper," her grandmother stated.

"I'm sorry, Grams. I'm not hungry. I won't be long." With that, Marlee ran out the door. She knew she was being rude to her grandmother, she just needed to talk to Miss Belle.

Belle was in the back and didn't hear Marlee come in. Marlee went over to the serving counter and made herself useful by straightening up. She didn't see Belle come through the door from the kitchen.

"Oh, Marlee, I didn't see you come in," Miss Belle said.

Marlee didn't look up or respond and tried to wipe her eyes without letting Miss Belle see her tears. She couldn't speak because of the lump in her throat.

"You can't hide your tears from me, Marlee," Miss Belle said gently. "Tell me what has happened."

"My mom went to the hospital today. She didn't know she was expecting, and she lost the baby. It was my sister."

"Oh, Marlee, I'm so sorry," Miss Belle told her.

"I've wanted a baby sister forever, but I gave up thinking I would get one. And now that I was going to get one, she's dead." Marlee started to sob.

"This is one of the hardest things for Christians to understand. Everyone misses out when a baby is lost, especially when it dies before it is even born. It seems a cruel act of nature to us that the unborn should not get a chance to live. The fact that it happens every day to millions of women doesn't make it easier. And I know that it's hard not to be angry when a mother loses her pregnancy only to see millions of other women deliberately ending theirs. It almost seems the ones that don't want their babies should be the ones to miscarry, and the ones that do should be able to carry them to term. But there's no explanation for it, and we won't know why until we see God face to face."

"She's in heaven right now," Marlee stated.

"Most assuredly she is, Marlee. The Bible says God knows each and every one of us and knew us before we were even conceived. That makes us a person as soon as we are conceived even though women try to deceive themselves that an unborn baby is not a human being until it is born. When does a human being get its soul, its uniqueness? Certainly not when it's born, and it's certainly not some magical moment while it's in the womb. It's right at the beginning when it is conceived.

"It happens by that unique combination from a mom and a dad. Nothing happens to the eggs of a woman, month after month as she sheds them. And nothing happens to the sperm of a man, month after month as he sheds them. But put one egg and one sperm together, and the miracle of life happens. The first man was made from dirt, and the first woman was made out of the side of man, but the first baby was created by the man and the woman together. That means God gave the job of continuing Creation to us.

"But the funny part is, once the baby starts growing, we have no control over it. Without the technology of today, we even have to wait for birth to know whether it's a boy or a girl. We don't even know that a pregnancy started. We have to wait for some signs to show up before we know it and then we have to take a test to be sure.

We should do everything we can to protect that process and consider all life sacred.

"But forgive me, Marlee, I didn't ask how your mom is doing?"

"I don't know how she feels about losing the baby. Physically, she is okay, but she had to have a transfusion, so they are not letting her come home for a day or two and then she has to be on bed rest."

"Is your daddy with her?"

"He will be tonight or rather sometime in the wee hours of the morning." Marlee wiped her tears with the back of her hand.

Miss Belle reached behind the counter to hand her a tissue. "Your mother may be sad for a while. We all have to trust God for the things we don't understand. He'll comfort us when we grieve. He is no stranger to sorrow you know."

"Yes, I know that God forsook Jesus when he was bearing all our sin," Marlee said.

"He also watched as his Son was brutally beaten, mocked, and spit upon by the very people he came to save, and even his best friends turned against him. I am glad I did not have to see my son die. I couldn't have stood it."

Marlee knew Miss Belle knew more than most what losing a child was like. "Oh, Miss Belle, I know you've been through a lot," Marlee said.

"Yes, that is so. It comforts me to know that Jesus suffered, though it hurts to know he didn't deserve it. You know he cried when his friend Lazarus died. Can you imagine being God, able to do all things, yet you cry because your friend died?"

"You always make me feel better, Miss Belle. That's why I came. Also, I came to tell you that Mama will be out of work for a week or so."

"Don't you worry about that. You concentrate on helping your mother."

"It's just that, well you know it's Christmastime, and you know what that means. Everybody needs a little extra. So, I was thinking, could I work for you after school?" Marlee asked, hoping Miss Belle would at least consider it.

"Oh, Marlee, you have such a heart of gold. You make your mama proud. And since I'm your unofficial grandmother, I'm very proud of you, too. Now listen up. We'll find a way to take care of your mama. I don't think she'd want you to neglect your studies."

Just then, Mrs. MacKinnon, the pastor's wife, came in with Mrs. Donnelly.

"Marlee, the pastor just told me about your mother. I am so sorry to hear what happened. I believe he is headed out to see you this evening. You give your family our love and tell them we will be praying for you," Mrs. MacKinnon said.

"Thank you, Mrs. MacKinnon, I will."

"And our love and prayers, too," Mrs. Donnelly said. "The mayor said to let him know if you need anything at all while your mother is in the hospital."

"Thank you, too, Mrs. Donnelly." She loved Mrs. Donnelly ever since she had been her Sunday school teacher when she was in grade school and Mrs. MacKinnon, too. Both of them were the nicest people you could meet.

"Betty and I thought we'd stop in, Belle, and offer to work Jenna Lee's shift until she can get back on her feet. So, you tell us what we need to do, and we'll do it," Mrs. MacKinnon said eagerly.

"Yes, I was a waitress before I married the mayor," Mrs. Donnelly stated.

"I'm afraid I have no such training, but I'm good with people. So, between the two of us, I figured we could cover for Jenna Lee, that way you could still afford to pay her. And hopefully we won't make a mess of things," said Mrs. MacKinnon. "We'll keep this joint jumpin'!"

Marlee laughed at Mrs. MacKinnon's funny expression. She couldn't believe they were willing to help her mother in that way.

"You tell your mama not to worry, we second stringers have come to help," Mrs. Donnelly told her.

"You'd really do that for her?" Marlee asked.

"Well, Belle hasn't said yes yet, but I don't know how she could say no. What do you say, Belle, two for the price of one!" Mrs. Donnelly looked at Marlee and winked.

"Okay, ladies, you have a deal, but I run a tight ship here, so when I say be here at three, I mean three." Marlee knew Belle was teasing them.

"I can't thank you all enough. I can't wait to tell Mom, it will mean a lot to her, and I know it will be a big relief to her, also," Marlee said gratefully.

"You just make sure she follows the doctor's orders. And she knows we both have been through it, so she can call us anytime if she needs a shoulder," Mrs. MacKinnon said.

"Thank you, Mrs. MacKinnon. And you, too, Mrs. Donnelly." Marlee was surprised to hear that both ladies had lost babies. She hoped she'd be able to talk to them about it. Maybe Mrs. MacKinnon could help her understand why the Lord let it happen, and she wanted to understand what her mother was going through. Marlee received hugs from all three ladies and left. She had to admit she felt better after her talk.

When she got home, she told her grandmother what Mrs. MacKinnon and Mrs. Donnelly were willing to do for her mom. Grams said that was wonderful and that she would call them to offer her thanks.

Marlee met Park upstairs, and he told her he'd just talked to Mr. Mosely who owned the gas station. "He's going to let me work a few hours a week, so I'll be able to give Mom some extra for Christmas."

"Oh, Park, now I know why you are my favorite brother."

"Huh. What would I be if I wasn't, your least favorite one?" They both laughed and felt that the sorrow lifted a little.

Marlee would have liked to help as well, but there weren't many babysitting jobs in town, and she couldn't get a real job at her age. She admired Jem who was out looking for chores but thought it was easier to find work if you were a boy. Marlee didn't believe Mr. Bascombe would have hired her to replace split rails and there wasn't an elderly lady who needed a companion. She decided she'd stick to her schoolwork and concentrate on her history project and help her mother around the house. She vowed to be the best Mary she could be and pray for a Christmas wish that would come true.

CHAPTER 11

Hope for the Future

Pastor MacKinnon knocked on the door of the Madison house, wishing it were under different circumstances. He was trying to find the right words to comfort and reassure the children.

Marlee opened the door, and the pastor could see she had been crying.

"Pastor Mac, come in. Your wife said you'd be stopping by. I saw her at Miss Belle's, and when I left, I thought I was doing better. I can't stop thinking about my sister. My grandmother is in the kitchen. I'll show you the way."

"I'll go upstairs and get Park," Marlee said to her grandmother who greeted the pastor and showed him to a seat at the table.

"I'm sorry your daughter has to go through this," he told her.

"You know, Pastor, I think every woman who either is going to be or wants to be a mother worries about whether she'll be able to carry her child to term. There are a lot of scary times during pregnancy. Some women seem to be able to get through nine months without batting an eye while others struggle the whole time. You'd think women would have adjusted by now to something that happens so often and to so many."

"Losing a life is never easy for the mother or the father," the pastor said, thinking about his own experience. "I'm sure the mother feels she failed in some way, and that is hard to deal with. Time helps, and some women find healing in trying again. Each woman handles it differently, and I suppose there are some who even feel relieved. There are no right or wrong emotions to something so personal. But remember, God can use any trial to help us grow in faith."

"Regret. I think that is what Jenna Lee expressed. She would miss experiencing life with this child, and Marlee wouldn't have the baby sister she has always wanted. Next spring, she will feel the empty arms that were supposed to be holding a precious little baby girl," Grams told him.

Parker and Marlee came into the room, and Marlee asked if they should sit down with them.

"Of course, take the seat next to me, Marlee." The pastor motioned to her to sit down.

"Do you want to go out to the living room? It's more comfortable to sit out there," Grams asked. "Park, please pour the pastor a cup of coffee before you sit down. I just made a fresh pot, Pastor."

"Thank you. This seat is fine," the pastor said as Park handed him a cup.

He poured milk in his coffee as Park sat down next to his grandmother.

"I know you kids are worried about your mom and no doubt about your dad, too. It's never easy for parents to lose a child, even one not born yet. Your mother may feel guilty and think she did something wrong."

"But I'm sure she didn't," Marlee said.

"No, she didn't, Marlee," the pastor said. "Feeling guilty is one of the stages of healing, and it's normal if she feels that way. I just want you kids to know in advance. She'll be sad, your dad too, but they will be all right. It takes time, but they will be all right. You know my wife and I went through it, and it's normal to ask why Jesus allows such things to happen."

"I talked to Miss Belle about that," Marlee said.

"You couldn't find a better person. Miss Belle lost the two most important people in her life, a husband and a son. Those are two of life's biggest challenges. I bet she didn't have an answer for you either," the pastor replied.

Marlee shook her head.

"The Bible says we must comfort those who are going through the same thing we did because we can share how the Lord comforted us. Paul says to remember that our present suffering cannot compare to what our future holds in glory, and Jesus said we should always glorify God in our trials. That is a strange concept, to praise God when we suffer so that God will be glorified. Most people think you should be mad at God and that it's his fault. But he gave us a perfect world in the beginning, and it was not his plan for us to experience suffering and death. And I can tell you personally, I don't know how anyone can go through suffering without Jesus by his side."

"I know that this isn't the end of the story. Everyone has to die, but there is life after that. It just seems so unfair when someone doesn't even get a chance to be born," Marlee stated. "Even though I know I'll see her in heaven."

"Concentrate on the eternity you will spend with her. You won't even remember that you didn't get to know her in this life," the pastor said as he patted her hand.

After they talked a little longer, the pastor said goodbye and told them he planned to go out first thing in the morning to visit with their parents in the hospital.

When he met with the Madisons the next morning, they seemed to be handling it well. Perhaps it was better that they had had no time to bond with the baby before they lost her. He made them promise to call him if they felt overwhelmed, especially Trent. When he was on the road, he would be alone with no one to talk to.

"Thank you for coming. Have you seen Marlee and Park? How are they taking it?" Jenna Lee asked. She was worried about her children, especially Marlee.

"Marlee is taking it a little harder than Park. He was pretty silent the whole time," the pastor commented.

"Yes, he suffers silently, and Marlee suffers openly, but I have found they both suffer about the same amount. Marlee has wanted a baby sister ever since she was little, though she quit mentioning it about four years ago," Jenna Lee told him.

"You know that Lucy and I went through this a few years ago. We're here to help in any way we can and of course to pray. It will get better," he said.

"Oh, I know. We'll get through it okay. I keep telling myself that I have two amazing kids already, and God knows best why this one didn't make it," Jenna Lee said.

"I'm trying to figure out how I can help her when I'm away so much," Trent said. "It's getting to be Christmastime when I have extra runs to make. I'll be away more than usual."

Trent worried about leaving his wife alone. It was hard enough to lose a child, harder still because it would soon be Christmas.

"It's okay, Trent," Jenna Lee assured him. "Besides, the doctor said I'll have to be on bed rest, and that will give me a chance to catch up on my crocheting. Pastor, I heard what Lucy and Betty are doing. I will thank them myself when I get a chance, but would you please tell your dear wife I cannot thank her enough for filling in for me."

The pastor nodded. They prayed together, and he took his leave.

On Sunday, Park and Marlee went to church with their grandmother. Marlee would remember the pastor's sermon for a long time to come:

"It is a common question after every catastrophe to ask why God allows terrible things to happen. I would like you to know I have no answer to that question. You can read in the book of Job when catastrophe befell him that his friends were quick to tell him that he must have sinned in some way. That is not the answer.

"In the New Testament, we are told that trials would come but that our faith should prevail because Christ has overcome the world. Paul tells us we have a responsibility to comfort those as we were comforted. Praise God that he is a God who does not want us to suffer alone. That is worthy of our praise. It is better that our suffering glorifies him rather than turn others away from him.

"All suffering is terrible, but I believe all suffering is relative. When you are suffering, there is no such thing as big versus small suffering, although I know some have a greater ability to bear suffering than others. And please don't think I am making light of anyone's suffering. Let me illustrate what I mean.

"I heard about a family that lost several children in a fire. I thought there was nothing more horrible and that no family should have to endure such a thing. But then I heard about a woman who left her husband and four children to go up the street to borrow something from a neighbor. While she was gone, her house burned down and all perished. I thought that was terrible and worse than the first family. Then I heard about a mother who left her twelve children alone at home, and a fire broke out, and they all perished. Now Job lost his ten children, all of his servants, and all of his wealth the same day. Not too long after that, he lost his health.

"If you look around, you will find suffering worse than yours, and you will find it lighter than yours. The truth is, sooner or later, we will all suffer, and believe me when we go through it, we suffer. When God first made Adam and Eve, there was no such thing as suffering. Wouldn't it be wonderful if it had stayed that way? Since it didn't, let me show you a different perspective. Most of us remember the horrible tsunami that took 250,000 lives in one day. How could God allow such an unspeakable tragedy to occur? He should have prevented it. So, let's pretend that God says, 'I agree with you. I will no longer allow that.'

"A new generation grows up, and they experience a horrible earthquake that takes 100,000 lives in one day. This is now the worst thing that has ever happened to mankind. How could God allow such an unspeakable tragedy to occur? He should have prevented it. So, let's pretend that God says, 'I agree with you. I will no longer allow that.'

"A new generation grows up, one that knows nothing of tsunamis or earthquakes. A hurricane occurs that takes 50,000 lives in one day. This is the worst thing that has ever happened to mankind. How could God allow such an unspeakable tragedy to occur? He should have prevented it. So, let's pretend that God says, 'I agree with you. I will no longer allow that.' A new generation grows up, one that knows nothing of hurricanes. I think you see my point. We can continue this scenario until we get God to eliminate disease, famine, weather events, shark attacks, bears, and alligators until we're left with mosquitoes and pimples. There will always be a 'worst thing that can happen to mankind' because we don't live in a perfect world.

"What should God expect in exchange for us to be able to live in a perfect world again? The Bible calls it obedience. Adam and Eve had one rule to follow, don't eat the fruit of that tree. As long as they obeyed, they would continue to live in a perfect world. It wasn't that this was the only tree from which to eat. None of us could have withstood that temptation. There was a garden full of trees, and it's not that the good trees tasted like broccoli and the forbidden one tasted like ice cream. The Bible says there was all manner of good eating in the Garden of Eden. Adam and Eve had one law to follow, and they didn't obey it. Along came Moses, and he gave us the Ten Commandments. Jesus summed up the ten into just two. How many of you have not broken one of the two?

"What would God expect in exchange for a perfect world? Perhaps he would require all seven billion of us on the planet to be perfectly obedient. We all know we would fail because we fail now. It wasn't hunger that caused Adam and Eve to eat the fruit. It was the desires of their hearts that did it. The same thing is true for us. It is the desires of *my* heart that take me away from the desires of God's heart.

"So, Adam and Eve exchanged a perfect world for a bite of fruit that they weren't even hungry to eat. We exchange the perfect world for the inability to obey God. The Bible says *all* have sinned and fallen short of obeying God. Face it. We have blown our chance for a perfect world in this life. And lest you say that God should be willing to give us a perfect world without requiring all to be obedient, may I remind you that someone else's disobedience would mess up my perfect world? The result is that we would accuse God of not punishing the disobedient while the rest of us agreed to live according to the rules. We would demand justice for disobedience.

"Where does the notion of Justice come from? For example, there are two boys. 'Boy one' shoots and kills 'boy two,' not accidentally but deliberately. 'Boy one' comes before the judge, and the evidence is overwhelming: 'boy one' is guilty. Both fathers are sitting in the courtroom, and the judge is ready to hand down the sentence. The father of 'boy one' hopes for mercy. The father of 'boy two' demands justice. There are two different perspectives. We are the ones that want mercy. God is the one that requires justice. If we choose Jesus, we get something better than mercy. It's called grace.

"Justice is when I'm guilty, and I deserve to be punished. That's all of us. Mercy is when I'm guilty, and I deserve to be punished, but I am let off the hook. Grace is when I'm guilty, but God declares that I am not guilty. What? That's right. I am guilty, no doubt about it. If I accept Jesus as my Lord and Savior, I not only receive mercy, I receive grace. The only way to live in a perfect world is to be perfect. Remember our spoilers out of the seven billion who refuse to be obedient. God is going to make a perfect world again. If I want to go to that perfect world, I have to be perfect. But I am a sinner, so I am not perfect. But when I accept Jesus, God gives me the perfection of Jesus, the only human who did live a perfect sin-free life. I get his perfection, and he gets my sin. That is grace. What a deal! Who in their right mind wouldn't take that deal?

"If you are going through suffering right now, I am sure this doesn't help. At least it doesn't make the suffering go away. But I am hoping you will get a new perspective on it. First that there are others who are suffering as you are, or maybe even worse than you are. Second, you will get through it. Job did, and God wants to help you through it. Third, help others who are suffering if you have been through the same thing they have. Fourth, if you haven't accepted Jesus's offer of grace, accept it today, and it's okay to long to live in that perfect world that is coming. Fifth, we are all going to die. We think of that as the ultimate suffering. But if you know Jesus, you never die. You merely end this life and begin the eternal one.

"Jesus can and will help you through your suffering. You may never understand why the 'bad thing' happened to you. You may never understand why your 'bad thing' is so much worse than someone else's 'bad thing.' You may be angry at God because he didn't keep the 'bad thing' from happening to you. I cannot answer the whys nor can anyone that I know.

"Ever hear of Horacio Spafford? He wrote the hymn, 'It Is Well With My Soul.' His son died before the Great Chicago Fire at the age of two. Spafford lost a lot of his money in that fire. He planned a trip to Europe with his family. Spafford had to send them on ahead and would join them once he settled a business matter that kept him from going with them. On the way over, the ship sank suddenly in a collision, and he lost all four of his daughters. His wife's telegram is now one of the most famous in the world; 'saved alone' it read. Spafford dropped everything to be at his wife's side. When the ship he took reached the spot of the disaster, he penned these words:

> When peace like a river attendeth my way,
> when sorrows like sea billows roll,
> whatever my lot, Thou hast taught me to say:
> it is well, it is well with my soul.

"If I have peace like a gently flowing river or sorrows like waves crashing over me, I must say, 'It is well with my soul.' Through the good and the bad, it is well with my soul. Why? Because Jesus has overcome this world and a perfect world is coming for me. Let us pray."

Marlee and Park returned home. Marlee knew the hymn well, they had sung it often in church. She hadn't heard the story behind it. Imagine writing those words while you were suffering that much tragedy. So much suffering. Even in this town, people had their struggles. She bet everybody had a sad story to tell of something they faced in life.

I'm growing up, she thought to herself. Thirteen would become fourteen, and one day, she would be an adult. For now, her mom and dad insulated her somewhat from the tragedies that happened in the world. Even Park was too young to remember the horrible tsunami that struck Indonesia in 2004, and neither of them was alive on September 11 when America was struck by terrorists.

No Christmas wish could wipe away all that suffering, which was what she wished would happen. How silly to think she could make a Christmas wish and Jem and Patrick and her family and all the others in Christmas that had troubles this time of year would have them magically solved. What we all really need is to be able to say, "It is well with my soul," when tragedy strikes and to thank God when we have peace like a river, she thought.

"It is well with my soul, God," Marlee told him.

CHAPTER 12

It's Beginning to Look a Lot Like Christmas

Marlee's mom came home the next day. The doctor said she would be fine and that there was no reason why she couldn't try again if she and her husband wanted a baby. But since this baby hadn't been planned, she and Trent didn't think they should since he was away from home so much. She asked Marlee and Park not to be too disappointed if there was no baby sister or brother in their future.

"Can we give her a name?" Marlee asked her mother.

She had been thinking a long time about this. No one would ever remember her "almost" baby sister, and since she was in heaven right now, she should have a name.

"Marlee, I think that's a wonderful idea. As a matter of fact, your dad and I discussed it, and he picked out the name Faith. What do you think?" Mrs. Madison said.

"I think it's perfect. I love it." What a perfect way to remember to have faith. "I love you, Mom," Marlee said, giving her mother a hug.

Park was his usual silent self the whole time, but Marlee knew he felt the same way she did. Park also believed it was well with his soul.

Meanwhile, Jem had gotten to see Mr. Trumbull who had been moved to a rehab center. He was getting better every day. He couldn't believe that Jem took the time to come all that way to see him. He was so happy to meet Jem's mother, Elisabeth, Elsa for short. Mr. Trumbull told her she should be very proud of her wonderful son. Jem beamed. *Mr. Trumbull remembered*, he thought.

After Elsa visited for a while, she told Jem it was time to go, so she went to bring the car around. After she left the room, Mr. Trumbull told Jem he was sorry he got sick and that Jem couldn't complete his yard work.

Elsa was kind enough to volunteer to drive Mr. Trumbull back to Christmas when he got released, which he hoped would be soon. Jem asked Mr. Trumbull who Rebecca was. Mr. Trumbull said that was his father's sister. Jem asked him if he knew about her Christmas wish, but he said his father never really talked about the Christmas celebration in his day, so he couldn't add anything to the story.

The whole town was now in full festival preparation, and you could see their efforts starting to come to life. Mrs. Madison was crocheting and actually considered her bed rest a blessing as now she could make extra items to sell. Elsa Jordan still came over to the Madison house most Saturdays to do her baking. She had been making some delicious fruitcakes, the ones southerners make best. Marlee thought she would fill out her thin frame if she sampled too many more of them.

One morning, Mayor Sam Donnelly was coming out of Belle's where he had stopped for a quick breakfast of oatmeal with a spoon of honey, sliced bananas, and his limit of one and a half cups of coffee, with cream but no sugar.

He'd left his house early to let his wife have a little more sleep since he knew she'd been out late. She and Belle had put up Christmas decorations last night. Their handiwork was evident because it was starting to look quite festive and Belle's shop window was a wonder. Mrs. Donnelly was coming back that evening to help Belle "hide" the ornaments that had her discount coupons taped to them. Festival attendees could hunt for these ornaments and use the coupons during their stay. As he stepped through the doorway, he nearly collided with Clara Pemberton.

"Oh, Clara, I'm glad I bumped into you although I'm glad I didn't literally bump into you," he laughed. "How do you think we're doing? No real glitches so far I hope."

"Well you know, Sam, I never think we have enough volunteers. I know the teams are hard at work, and we're meeting next Saturday to see where we are. You're welcome to come if you want," she told him.

"I wish I could, but Betty has promised me to Belle. I have to put her lights up, and I haven't even started the lights on Town Hall." Suddenly, there was a din of beeping horns, and he looked at the street to find out what was going on.

"You know there's a lot more noise than usual. I don't like to hear all this honking in town. We didn't use to have this much traffic and noise in the morning," he said.

"You know they just opened a mega mall in Henderson," Miss Pemberton said. "Everyone's going out there because their stores open so early. They have some excellent sales going on right now for the opening, and it's not even Thanksgiving yet. Have you heard how many chain stores are going to be open Thanksgiving night? I guess if one does then they all must. You know there's a Black Friday, and now they started having Cyber Monday."

"Yes, Clara, and it worries me because every time a new mall opens, I wonder how long we'll be able to hang on. We can't compete with their extended hours and who in town would think to open Thanksgiving night? I'm worried that the day will come when shopping will compete with Festival attendance, and I'm not even sure we'll see the level of participation this year that we've had in years past," the mayor said. He was clearly concerned about these new developments.

"I know, Sam. Young people are turning away from Christmas traditions, and Christmas is becoming more and more secular every year. I'm even surprised we are still allowed to have our Nativity Night. But remember, those stores might have the goods, but they don't have the service," she said trying to encourage him.

"True enough, but I'm afraid they won't want to come out all this way for our service. You know, if we start seeing a drop in festival revenue, some of our shops might have to close. Plenty of small towns have become ghost towns. I hope we don't become one of them. Maybe we should start thinking of some new events we can add next year to get a bigger draw."

"Don't be too pessimistic, Sam. We are still *the* destination at Christmastime," she said with enthusiasm.

"I hope it stays that way. Well, it's good to hear all this hammering, at least. As you said, we must not procrastinate. Our Christmas preparations appear to be well underway."

With that, the mayor headed toward Town Hall and Miss Pemberton made her way to the library. Today, she would see if she could get all the lights out and untangled so they could be hung up. Miss Pemberton had enlisted Tim Johnson's help later in the morning, so she needed to hurry up.

As she passed each shop, she noticed more and more windows were being decorated, and she wondered if each shop owner was trying to outdo his neighbor. It looked like some serious effort was going into these windows. Maybe they should have a window decorating contest and attendees could vote for their favorite. She made a note to remember that for the next meeting. She didn't think it could be added to this year's schedule, but it was something to consider for next year. *We've been adding so many events every year that if it keeps up, we'll have to start planning in July,* she thought. But it was fun, and it did bring revenue into town.

Now that they had to compete with more stores and later shopping hours, they would have to come up with more ways to attract the crowds. *It will be a long time before anyone in Christmas opens on Thanksgiving, though. What is this world coming to?* she said to herself.

CHAPTER 13

Hayden and Hudson

M arlee finally caught up with Hayden as they were entering the girl's lavatory. She had been meaning to ask Hayden about her Christmas wish since she had played Mary last year. This was the first time their paths crossed. Hayden was a grade ahead, so she and Marlee shared no classes. Since Hayden and her twin brother, Hudson, rode the bus, there wasn't any time after school.

Marlee knew the Hamiltons were among the least well-off families in the area. They lived in a trailer park near the campgrounds outside of town. Hayden's clothing was well-worn, and Marlee knew she occasionally wore the same outfit more than once during the week. People in town did not think the worst of them because of their circumstances.

Both Hayden and Hudson were among the smartest kids in school. Hayden always won the spelling bee in grade school, and they were both straight A students in middle school, and Hayden was, well there was no other way to put it, a beautiful girl.

Marlee had wanted to be friends with Hayden, but because she was a year older and lived outside of town, it was hard for Marlee to find time even to talk to her.

"Hayden, wait up. Can I talk to you a minute? Are you crying? Hayden, what's the matter?" Marlee asked.

Hayden quickly wiped the tears away. "No, I'm not crying. I just had something in my eye."

"Hayden, please, I've always wanted to be a friend, and I'm sorry we haven't been, please let me know. I'd like to help if I can."

"There's nothing you can do," Hayden responded.

"But, Hayden, I'm Mary this year and I—"

"Are you talking about that stupid Christmas wish nonsense?" Hayden asked as she turned to face Marlee.

"Well, I thought—"

"Marlee, I appreciate that you want to help. But that wish legend is a bunch of baloney. Was I Mary last year? Do you think my wish came true? It's all rubbish."

"What was your wish, may I ask you that much?" Marlee asked.

"If you have to know, I wished my dad would find a job. You'd think if there were anyone who should have a wish granted it would be my dad. All those years at the factory and now nothing. Two years he's been looking and nothing, and now his unemployment runs out this month, one month before Christmas, can you believe that?"

Marlee reached into her purse. She had a five-dollar bill that Miss Belle had given her last Christmas. That's how long Marlee had held on to it. When she thanked Miss Belle, she told her she would only spend it on something very special, and nothing had ever come up that was special enough.

"I know it's not much, but please, take this," Marlee said as she handed her the bill.

"I don't want your money or your pity."

"It's not my money," Marlee said matter-of-factly.

"What do you mean?" Hayden said, confused.

"It's the Lord's money. I give it to you in the name of the Lord. So, you have to take it because that's how it works."

Hayden looked at the five-dollar bill. She knew that even that small amount could make a difference. At least, it would mean her mom could set another meal on the table.

"If you take it though, it's not really a gift," Marlee explained.

"What do you mean?" Hayden asked.

"Well, if you thought that I gave you this money out of pity, it wouldn't be praise money. God is not about pity, he's about praise. So, there's a string attached. That way you'll know it's not pity money."

"What string?" Hayden was really confused. Was Marlee giving her the money or not?

"You must promise me that tonight you will praise God for giving your dad a job," Marlee said.

"But my dad doesn't have a job."

"That sounds like you pity him because he doesn't have a job," Marlee said.

"I pity all of us, to tell you the truth," Hayden said.

"That's why this is praise money. So, start praising God for giving your dad a job. Let's do it now," Marlee said.

"I don't know how to pray. We don't go to church."

"So, you think you have to go to church before you can pray? We'd all be in trouble if God worked that way. Come on over here with me." Marlee took her over to the corner.

"Here, hold onto this five-dollar bill, and bow your head. I'll pray the words. Tonight, you do the same thing when you get home, okay?" Hayden nodded and bowed her head.

"Dear Father, all good things come from you. As Hayden holds this five-dollar bill, which is praise money, I want to thank you for the job that Hayden's dad is going to get. And Father, because you know what a hard worker he is, please give him a better job than the one he lost. We praise you for the answers to this prayer. In Jesus's name. Amen."

Hayden was getting ready to tell Marlee she was crazy, but then she suddenly stopped and instead said, "Thank you, Marlee. You know that's the nicest thing anyone has done for me in a long time."

"I hear Hudson is one of the three kings this year," Marlee said, changing the subject.

"That's right. Marlee. If anyone deserves to have their Christmas wish come true, it's you. You have a good heart."

"Thank you, Hayden. That's one of the nicest things anyone has said to me in a long time. If you ever decide you want to come to church, look for me, and we can sit together."

"Thanks, Marlee. I'll let my mom know. She's not really one for going to church, but maybe she'll let me come one day."

"If you need us to pick you up or something, I'm sure my mom wouldn't mind coming out your way."

Marlee and Hayden left the bathroom, and each girl went back to her classroom. When school was over, Hayden and Marlee saw each other in the crowd, and Marlee put her hands together in prayer to remind her. Hayden gave her the thumbs up sign.

Marlee thought she might change her Christmas wish, but in the next few days, she put the incident out of her mind and truth be told, she forgot all about it.

Several days later, Hayden approached her as Marlee sat down in the cafeteria.

"Marlee," Hayden greeted her.

"Hayden. Oh, I'm glad to see you. Did you remember to pray?" Marlee felt a little sheepish as she hadn't followed up with her own prayers for Mr. Hamilton.

"Yes, and a funny thing happened. No, it's not my dad, no job yet. But let me tell you, I did pray that night, and I've been praying since. Instead of being stressed and worried, I have this calmness. Like somehow everything's going to be okay," she told Marlee.

"Oh, Hayden, do you know what that is?"

"No. You know about it?" Hayden said, surprised that Marlee understood what she had experienced.

"I do. That's God's peace. See, he gives us peace that passes all understanding. That means when logically you shouldn't have peace, but you do anyway. Look at it this way. Everybody in the whole world who had a dad out of work at Christmastime would be worried and fearful about the future, right? That's the normal response," Marlee said, and Hayden nodded.

"But instead of being worried and fearful, you have a sense of peace that things are going to be okay in the end, right?" Hayden nodded again. "But that's not normal to feel that way. That's because you feel God's peace. Humans don't have peace in a storm. They only have peace when it's peaceful, and it's a good thing to keep praying and praising God for the job he's going to give your dad," Marlee explained.

"I gave my mom the five-dollar bill and told her it was praise money and not pity money. Marlee, she cried, but do you know what? Somehow, we've been able to eat for a whole week with that five dollars. So, thank you, from the bottom of my heart, and my mom thanks you, too."

They gave each other a hug and Hayden had to hurry to her next class. Marlee wished she had another five-dollar bill to give to Hayden. She made a mental note to ask Pastor Mac next Sunday if there was any money in the benevolent fund that they could spare for the Hamilton family. Maybe they could give them something until that job came through because Marlee knew it had to be on its way.

CHAPTER 14

Danger Ahead

"We just have to find that gold!" Marlee exclaimed to Patrick and Jem as she reached the second floor of the library.

"Marlee, what are you talking about?" Patrick said while Jem said, "Marlee, you're crazy."

Both boys dropped what they were doing as Marlee approached them.

"What *are* you talking about?" Patrick asked again.

"I don't think anyone has ever made a systematic attempt to look for clues to where Jedediah left his gold," Marlee responded.

"But people have been looking for that gold for a hundred and fifty years, and we don't know if it's still there," Jem added.

"Correct, but we don't know that it is *not* there," Marlee answered him.

"How are we going to find the time? We have to finish our projects and start working on Nativity Night, and I've got stuff to do at home. Besides, Mr. Trumbull will be home soon, and I have to help him out," Jem said.

"What's up with you and Mr. Trumbull anyway?" Patrick said.

He couldn't believe anyone would waste his time helping that guy out. Everybody knew what a mean old man he was.

"You remember the reason I borrowed your bike?" Jem asked.

"Yeah, I remember," Patrick replied.

"Mr. Trumbull said I could do some chores for him, but then he got sick, and I'm really behind. I wanted to get the stove for

Christmas, but now I'm not going to have enough money, and it's too cold to work outside. Besides, his house isn't haunted; it's just run down, and he's not a mean man, he really is nice," Jem explained.

"So, what's your plan, Marlee? How do we get started? I don't know how to look for 150-year-old clues," Patrick asked.

"Patrick, did you ever find out where Smith's land was located?" Marlee asked him.

"No. I've looked at all the maps, and nothing has his name on it. He's not in the deed book or the plat book either," Patrick told her.

"Miss Pemberton says she found his cabin once. You go behind the church and straight up the mountain," Marlee told them.

"You want to find the cabin?" Jem asked.

"I think that's where we should start. It would be so much easier if we had a map showing where it was," Marlee said, disappointed that Patrick hadn't been successful locating the Smith cabin on the map.

"When do you want to go?" Patrick asked.

"Well, there's no time like the present," Marlee said with a big smile.

"Seriously, you want to go now?" Jem asked.

"We've got about five hours of daylight left. All we have to do is go straight up the mountain. If we don't find anything, we come back down and try again later," Marlee said.

"I'm in," Jem said. "I was hoping you wanted to try and find his place, and I could go with you. But do you think Liam and Park should go with us? You know, they've had more experience marking trails."

"Yes, I'll go home and get Park. Will you go get Liam, Patrick? Can you meet back here in half an hour? And have him bring some food, water, and a flashlight. Jem, will you be warm enough in that jacket? I can bring you one from home," Marlee asked him.

"This one's okay. We'll be home before sundown, right? My mom doesn't like it if I'm out after dark," Jem replied.

"Yeah, we'll be back before sundown. Up and right back if we don't find anything," Marlee assured him.

Park took some convincing and told Marlee straight to her face that this was a hairbrained idea. They let their mom know they were going out and would be back before dinner. Park packed a few things in his school backpack, mostly bags of chips and Cheetos, which he thought would keep him until supper. He didn't think to bring water, but Marlee grabbed her water bottle out of the fridge. She decided to bring her winter gloves just in case they had to move any logs or rocks when they got to the cabin. She was optimistic that they would find it.

When the five of them reassembled at the library, they set off for the churchyard. Just as they were leaving, Marlee found Miss Pemberton and told her they were going to look for Smith's cabin. "Straight up the mountain, right?" Marlee asked.

"Yes, and before you crest it, you'll find a rather large clearing. As I remember, the cabin is right in the center."

"Thanks, Miss Pemberton," Marlee said as she raced out the door.

After an hour hiking, Marlee didn't think they'd made much progress. Going straight up sounded a lot easier than it was. There was no trail, so they had to follow whatever openings they could find in the thick underbrush. There were lots of fallen trees, many of which they had to go around, and large outcroppings of rock that were too steep to climb. That required further detours. Liam remembered to mark the trails, but he wasn't sure how visible his marks would be on the return trip.

Two hours into the trip, Marlee thought they were finally making progress. They arrived at a spot that was more thinned out than what they had encountered so far. Marlee spotted a huge old oak tree at the edge of the small clearing and discovered the initials, "JCS," clearly carved into the bark.

"Look at this!" she called out. They all rushed over to see what she had found.

"Wow, initials," Jem said, a hint of sarcasm in his voice.

"That's great, Marlee, but we're looking for a cabin," Park said.

"Yes, I know, but it means we're getting close," Marlee said.

She didn't understand why no one else was excited.

"Let's keep going," Liam advised.

"Who's keeping track of the time?" Patrick asked, but he didn't get a response.

After a pause, Liam said, "Don't worry, Patrick. The return trip will go much faster since we'll be going downhill. I figure we have about an hour and a half before we have to start back."

"Hey, does that look like a trail?" Jem said, pointing to what looked like a small path.

"I think it is," Liam said. "It's pretty overgrown, but it does look like it's been used before. Listen, you guys, stay put while I see if it leads anywhere. I'll come back for you if it looks promising."

Everyone thought this was a good idea and that it would save time. There was no sense in everyone going if they just ended up turning around.

"I'll go with you, Liam," Park said.

It was about fifteen minutes later when they returned. It did look promising. They all followed behind the two older boys, and forty-five minutes later, they came to a clearing. It was quite over-grown, but it was a clearing nonetheless, and in the middle of it, they found the remains of an old cabin.

"I don't believe it, we did it!" Marlee exclaimed.

They all rushed over to examine what was left of the cabin.

"What exactly are we looking for?" Jem asked.

"Why don't you and Patrick walk around the perimeter? Look for any markings like rock formations that don't look natural or carvings in the trees," Liam suggested.

"What are you going to do?" Patrick asked his brother.

"Well, I'm hungry, so I'm going to grab a snack," Liam said.

"I'm hungry, too," Patrick said.

"Okay, all of you who want to take a snack break, come over here. There's a fallen tree we can sit on," Liam suggested.

All the boys wanted a snack, but Marlee was too excited to eat. She was still systematically looking and moving debris out of the way when she finally found something.

The cabin indeed had been nearly demolished, and it was hard to tell whether it had been done by humans or nature. You could still see the remnants of two walls, but the other two were gone entirely. All that remained was a pile of rotted leaves and wood. What roof there had once been was long gone. The only way you could tell it had once been a person's home, was that it had a stone fireplace. Much of the hearth was still standing, but many of the chimney stones had been scattered everywhere. A lot of the logs were still recognizable, but they'd been dragged around.

I guess people thought they would find gold in the walls, Marlee thought to herself.

There were vines, leaves, and weeds everywhere, and Marlee could see that insects were helping to return the logs back to the soil. They scurried away every time she moved their covering. *It's more of a mess than I expected,* Marlee thought to herself. It would have been a good idea if someone had preserved this place before this much damage was done.

It was the log that just didn't look like the rest of them that got her attention.

"I think I found something!" she called out. The boys raced over to see.

"Help me dig it out. Here, Liam, take this end, please." Liam took one end, and Marlee gave hers to Park. The log was quite heavy, and Liam and Park were having trouble lifting it up.

"Liam, did you bring a flashlight?" Marlee asked.

"Yes. Patrick, go get it out of my backpack," Liam said.

"Park, look at this," Liam said. "Jem, bring that bottle of water."

Marlee held the flashlight while Jem poured a little water over the mud on the log. Marlee thought she saw some carvings. "Look here, is this something carved into the log?" she asked them.

"Yeah, I see it. Bring the flashlight closer," Liam responded.

The five of them were too excited to notice that time was slipping away. Marlee took a tissue out of her pocket and was able to clean off the center of the log. It showed that at one time, it had been polished, unlike the other logs which were rough looking.

"Can you make anything out? All I see is what looks like an 'M' and an 'I,'" she said.

"That looks like an eight to me," Patrick said, pointing to what looked like a number.

"I think it's a six," Jem stated.

"Is there anything we can put on it to give it more contrast?" Marlee asked.

"Chalk maybe," Patrick said.

"Are you nuts? Where are we going to find chalk up here?" Jem questioned.

"How about charcoal then," Patrick stated. He was only trying to be helpful. "If we could find the remnants of an old fire, there might be a piece."

Each of them looked for any signs of a fire left behind by a previous searcher. If anyone noticed they were losing daylight, no one said anything. They were too caught up in their excitement.

"I found a piece!" Jem exclaimed, and everyone turned back to the log to see if the charcoal idea would work.

"Rub it gently. Here let me do it." Park took over. "Shine a light for me. I need to see if I can get any contrast." He tried rubbing back and forth, but the charcoal didn't make any dust and was only breaking off in pieces. "Maybe if we had ashes it would work. This piece is too hard and worn. It's not working."

"We can't drag this thing home. Any other ideas?" Liam asked.

"How about if we each run our fingers over it. Don't say anything until everyone has a try. That way we can get each person's impression about what it is," Park suggested.

"That's a great idea, Park. I'll go first." Marlee slowly ran her fingers over each of the marks but only came away with what she initially thought. The first mark was the letter M. There was a second mark, but she couldn't tell whether it was an I or a T or an L. The only other marking was a six.

After the group all gave their opinions, they only agreed that the first letter was an M. There was one number, but they were divided as to whether it was a six or an eight. Two of them thought there was a number one after that, but the rest of them thought it was just a slight ridge in the wood.

"It's not much of a clue," Park remarked, wondering why he had given up a Saturday afternoon to come out here for nothing.

"It might be if we could read it," Marlee said, not ready to give up. She'd ask Miss Pemberton, perhaps she was familiar with the markings or had heard something about it in her lifelong study of the town's history. "I should have taken you up on your snack offer. Is there anything left? I'm hungry."

"I emptied my backpack," Liam said.

"Sorry, Sport. We ate everything I brought," Park added.

"Hey, guys, has anyone been keeping track of the time? It looks like we're losing the sun," Patrick said with a tinge of worry in his voice.

"Yeah, and I'm getting cold. We've got to hurry. I should have taken you up on your offer for another jacket, Marlee. Why would a guy want to live way up here away from everything? You'd think if he started a town, he'd want to live in it," Jem remarked.

"If you knew the right way to get here it wouldn't take more than forty minutes or so. It's just because we didn't know the way that it took so long. Plus, it's overgrown after a hundred years. You'll see. I bet we're down the mountain in half an hour," Liam said.

He was probably right about Jedediah Smith's ability to find his way up, but he was sure wrong about their ability to find the way down.

As they made their way down the mountain, they were unable to find Liam's markings because it was too dark to see anything under the tree cover. They tried using the flashlight, but nothing looked familiar in the dark. Liam had them turn it off to save the battery strength in case they really needed it later. It wasn't time to start panicking. He and Park had to keep the younger ones from getting scared. He hoped they didn't hear any worry in his voice.

"I don't think this is the way we came," Patrick said.

"Yeah, why is it taking so long? Shouldn't we have gotten to that small clearing by now?" Marlee asked.

"I'm really getting cold, guys. Are you sure this is that old trail?" Jem was getting scared, and he was ready to let everyone know it. He kept muttering to himself, *My mom is going to kill me.*

"What do you think we should do, Liam?" Park asked in a low voice so that the others wouldn't hear. "Should we try to turn around and go back to the cabin and start again?"

"No, as long as the terrain is heading downhill, we'll be okay. Wherever we come out, we'll be able to find our way back to town."

So, the five of them continued on, but about twenty minutes later, Liam and Park realized that the terrain had changed, and they were no longer going downhill. Liam left them and tried to find where the ground led down, but it was too dark, and the trees were very thick. The underbrush made it difficult to see anything. "Give me the flashlight, and I'll see if I can find a way out of this." He had been gone for about ten minutes. Park could tell he was worried when he returned.

Patrick and Jem were starting to get scared, Patrick less so because at least he had his big brother with him. Liam had been a top-notch Boy Scout. Jem still muttered, *My mom is going to kill me.*

"Did anyone else bring a flashlight?" Liam asked, but no one else thought to bring one since they were all supposed to be home before dark.

"I definitely wore the wrong jacket," Jem muttered. "My mom is going to kill me."

Marlee grabbed Park by the arm. "We're lost, aren't we?"

Park nodded his head.

CHAPTER 15

Worried Parents

Jenna Lee Madison was getting concerned. It was now past dark, and the kids should have been back nearly an hour ago. She phoned Elsa Jordan to see if Jem knew where Marlee might have gone.

"Hi, Elsa? It's Jenna Lee. Is Jem there? Marlee and Park went out and were supposed to be back by now. Maybe Jem knows where they were going," she asked.

"Oh Jenna Lee, I'm frantic. Jem's not here either. He knows he's not supposed to be out after dark. I have no idea where he is," Mrs. Jordan responded.

"Okay, don't panic. Let me find out if Molly knows anything. I'll call you back."

She called the O'Brien's phone number, and Collin answered.

"It's Jenna Lee. Collin, are Patrick and Liam there? I'm looking for Marlee and Park, and I think Jem might be with them. Maybe Patrick knows where they were going?"

"You, too? That makes all five of them missing," he said. "I think we need to call Sheriff Cooper. I'll head over to your house and alert the sheriff on the way. He'll help us figure out what to do next. Hang on, I'm sure they're not far. There's not that much trouble they can get into around here."

"Okay, I'll see if Elsa can come over here, too. Thanks, Collin."

Jenna Lee called Elsa back, but she said she would stay put since she didn't want to upset Gracie. "Call me back when you find them. Please, Lord, let them be found."

She hung up the phone, hoping that there was a simple explanation for why they were missing. She thought about the Trumbull house. Even though he was still out at the rehab center, maybe they all went out there. She called Jenna Lee back immediately.

"I thought of something. Can someone run out to the Trumbull house? Maybe they all went out there for some reason...no, Mr. Trumbull is still at the center...okay thanks, Jenna Lee. Call me back as soon as you know."

Twenty minutes later, the phone rang, and the news was disappointing. Collin told Jenna Lee that he found the house completely dark and empty. By the time he returned, Sheriff Cooper had arrived and was assembling a search team. Jenna Lee called Elsa back to let her know. "Are you sure you don't want to wait here, Elsa?" she asked again.

"I'll come as soon as Gracie goes to bed, and I can get a sitter. I don't want to upset her if I can help it," Elsa said.

The Sheriff was trying to calm them all down. "I'm sure there is a logical reason for why they are late. There's no need to worry yet. What do we know about where they were headed?"

"Park told me they were going out and would be back before dinner," Jenna Lee told him. "They didn't say where they were going."

"Liam and Patrick didn't say anything at all to me. I thought Patrick was at the library with Marlee and Jem," Mrs. O'Brien said.

"Let me get ahold of Clara. Maybe they said something to her," Sheriff Cooper said.

Miss Pemberton had just left the library and did not hear the phone ringing inside. She decided not to hurry home. Her trip usually took about ten minutes, but she wanted to look at all of the Christmas windows that had been decorated. They really were impressive. She had asked the festival committees if they wanted to add a window decorating contest to the list of events. Everyone was enthusiastic even though it would require a lot of additional work. They agreed it was too much to take on for this year, but they were looking forward to a little friendly competition next year.

The sheriff rang Clara's home phone, but she wasn't there either. He radioed headquarters and asked for someone to drive around to see if they could find her. "Get back to me right away."

"10-4," the radio crackled.

The women went into the kitchen to pray. Collin asked the sheriff what he really thought. Since Trent was still on the road, he was the only father present. "Tell me the truth, what do you think the odds are of us finding them?"

"I know you're worried, Collin, but it's way too early to panic. I need you to stay calm for the women's sake. As soon as we reach Clara, we'll figure out what to do next. My deputies are forming a search team, and they're contacting other jurisdictions to see if we can get more volunteers. Oh, hold on."

"James, what have you got? Say that again?" the sheriff said into his radio.

Molly was concerned that Jenna Lee shouldn't be out of bed. With the stress of worrying for Marlee and Park, she could see she was ailing. "Jenna Lee, we can wait in your bedroom as easily as out here. You get back in bed, and I'll make us a cup of tea and a pot of coffee for the men."

"Oh, thank you, Molly. I have to try to reach Trent," Jenna Lee said.

"Wait until we know a little more before calling him. After all, they may come walking through the door at any moment," Molly replied.

"Molly, you are a dear friend. I need a level head thinking for me right now." Jenna Lee did think she needed to lie down and was grateful Molly had come.

Miss Pemberton was surprised to hear someone calling her name. At first, she thought she was mistaken, but then she turned and saw a squad car pulled up to the curb with the window rolled down. It was Deputy James. She couldn't imagine what trouble she had caused.

"Deputy James, what is wrong?" she asked him.

"Did the Madison kids tell you where they were going when they left the library?"

"Oh my, let me think," she told him.

What was it Marlee said? That's right, she asked me how to get to the Smith cabin, she thought to herself.

"Yes, Officer James, Marlee said she was going to find Smith's cabin," Miss Pemberton told him.

"Do you remember what time that was?"

She answered that she thought it was about noon.

"Thanks, Miss Pemberton."

He drove away so quickly that Miss Pemberton barely heard him say thanks. *Oh my!* she thought. *I hope they have not gotten into trouble up there.*

Sheriff Cooper heard the radio crackle with the message. "All right, James. Ask Pastor Mac to get over to the church and open it up for us. Then get as many volunteers assembled as you can and meet me there. That's where we'll set up our command post. I need you to round up some blankets and water. And something hot for them to drink. And coffee for us. I don't know how long this night is going to last." He turned to Collin and said, "They went up on Smith's Mountain looking for the cabin."

"I'm going with you," Collin said.

Jenna Lee heard them from the hallway. "Take Sox with you. He'll find Marlee, he can find Marlee anywhere."

Temperatures had been dropping since nightfall. They really had something to worry about now.

CHAPTER 16

The Rescue

"Guys, we're going to stop here and try to light a fire. Everyone, empty your pockets. Let's hope we find something we can start a fire with." Liam knew there was a small chance he could get a spark from the flashlight, but he didn't want to have to short it out to start a fire. He knew they might need it for a signal and it was losing strength quickly.

"I've got matches!" Park shouted. "Oh, my goodness!"

"Oh, thank you, Lord, that Park is a pack rat. I bet they've been in there since our fishing trip on my birthday. I will never criticize you again, Park."

Marlee was praising God he never cleaned out his backpack. Hers was always neat and orderly, and she couldn't understand why he just kept shoving more things in his. Now she was grateful he never listened to her.

There were only three matches left, so Liam had them scurrying around to find anything that would burn. Park had a lot of paper to use, but they didn't want to light the fire until they'd found some dry leaves and kindling-sized branches. If they lit the paper on fire, it would burn out too quickly and waste a match.

It was hard finding anything in the dark, and unfortunately, they didn't have much moonlight. The three younger ones eventually came back with an armful of leaves and twigs, so Liam lit the fire. It took on the first try, thanks to Park's scrap paper.

"Just think, Sport, you're getting your wish," Park teased his sister.

"And what is that, Park?" Marlee responded.

"My backpack is cleaned out."

Ordinarily, she would have laughed at this, but now they were concentrating on how to stay warm through the night, especially Jem, who was only wearing a light jacket.

"We need to offer up a praise prayer," Marlee said. "You all bow your heads, and let's hold hands, and I'll say it."

Everyone's hands were freezing cold. Marlee was still wearing her gloves, which had gotten wet moving logs and rocks back at the cabin, so her hands were just as cold as theirs.

"Father, I praise you because our rescuers are on their way. I know you know just where they are, and you certainly know where we are because you can see us huddled here by this fire. Help them to find us quickly, and would you please send Jem some extra warmth? And, Lord, tell my mom to send Sox with them because I know he can find me wherever I am. He's the best dog ever, Lord and thanks for bringing him into our family. And we praise you for keeping our fire going. In Jesus's name," and they all said, "Amen."

Liam was worried about the fire and hoped God would answer her prayer. He knew without finding a lot more wood, it was not going to last through the night.

"Oh my goodness, did anyone tell somebody where we were going? I know we didn't," Liam said as he just realized he hadn't told his parents where they were going.

"We just told Mom we were going out and would be back for dinner," Park said.

"Don't look at me. My mom thinks I'm at the library, and she's gonna—"

"Yes, we know, Jem. She's going to kill you," Marlee finished his thought. "Oh wait, wait! I told Miss Pemberton we were coming up to find the cabin."

"That's the second miracle we need to thank the Lord for," Liam said.

"What's the first?" Jem asked.

"The matches," Liam responded. "Park, see if you can get some more wood, maybe something a little larger that will burn longer. I think this fire is hot enough that a branch will take."

If they could put some larger logs on the fire, they had a better chance of making it last through the night, and it would give off more heat.

"And, you guys, see if you can find any good-sized rocks," Liam directed. "If we surround the fire with them, we might be able to warm ourselves with rocks if the fire doesn't last all night. At least the rocks will keep us warm for a little while." Jem got up to go also. "Not you, Jem. You're shivering, and I want you to stay by the fire. See if you can get a little closer."

By now, everyone was afraid when Liam said "all night" as none of them had ever been overnight in November temperatures without a sleeping bag and better clothing. Marlee thought some pine boughs might at least be made into a windbreak, so she gathered up what she could find and brought them back.

"Good idea," Liam praised her. "Let's see if we can build a wall of them. It will help keep some of the wind off of us."

The only thing left in Park's backpack was a hunting knife. He cut down some fresh boughs. They made a pretty good wall, and it actually did work a little. *Better than nothing,* they all thought.

"Nobody can go to sleep," Liam stated. "And we're going to have to try to keep Jem warm as best we can. If you feel yourself getting sleepy, tell the person next to you. We have to avoid hypothermia, or we'll go down fast, and let's try to be quiet and listen for any sounds. I don't want to scare you, but we have to be alert. There are bears and wolves in these mountains. Park and I will stand watch, but I still don't want you going to sleep. And, everybody, listen very carefully. The fire will help them find us."

"How? It's too little, and no one will see it," Patrick said.

"They'll smell it," Liam answered.

"That's our third miracle," Marlee said.

"What is?" Liam asked.

"That we brought you along," Marlee said.

She thanked God for Liam and what he knew about surviving in the elements.

Time passed very slowly for the group of five, and it was getting darker and colder. They huddled around the fire, and every now and again had to back away from the smoke that blew in their faces. They resupplied the wood about every half hour and had been able to put a couple of good-sized logs on to keep it burning.

"Marlee, are you still awake?" She could hear the concern in Park's voice.

"Yes, I was just thinking how sorry I am that I got you all into this."

"Yeah, maybe I can get my mom to kill you instead," Jem quipped, and everyone laughed this time.

"Is everybody hanging in there?" Liam asked. He heard a lot of chattering teeth but managed to hear everyone say yes. "I never thought to ask, did anyone wear a watch?"

This time, he heard a chorus of nos. Liam figured it must be about nine o'clock. "They should be coming soon. If they started missing us at six, I figure it would take an hour before they raised the alarm."

"I hope they brought Sox. He'll be able to follow our trail, and they'll get here a lot quicker than it took us," Marlee said

"Park, keep stoking the fire. I'm going for more wood," Liam told him.

Liam came back in about five minutes with another armful of wood. *I sure hope we can make this fire last,* he thought to himself. *I don't want to have to venture too far into the woods for more wood.*

They spent another hour huddling around the fire and occasionally got up to do jumping jacks to keep their bodies warm. Everyone had grown very silent, and all that could be heard was Liam's occasional, "Is everybody awake?"

"I thought I heard a dog barking!" Patrick had been straining his ears to listen ever since Liam said, "they should be here shortly."

"I don't hear anything," Park said. "Which direction do you think?"

Patrick couldn't be sure, so they settled back a few more minutes, and everyone strained their ears.

It was Marlee who heard the next bark. "I hear it. It must be Sox."

Liam asked if she could tell which direction and she pointed.

"I'm going to go down that direction. Hand me the flashlight. Maybe I can make a signal the search party will be able to see. Don't anybody start yelling, it might give off too many echoes if they aren't close enough yet," Liam told them.

Liam took the flashlight and tried to shine it high in the trees, hoping that the search party might see the light. He listened intently and was sure he heard calling and a dog barking. "Dad!" he shouted. Maybe his single word would have a chance of being heard. He was still worried his cry might echo off the neighboring mountain.

In a few more minutes, he could tell the search party was getting closer. "Over here!" The four others found him and started calling, too.

"Sh," he said to quiet them. Liam heard his father clearly call his name. "All of you go back to the fire. They'll hear me. I want you to stay as warm as possible until they get here."

"Dad, over here!" Liam yelled.

A few minutes later, there was a loud rustling sound in the bushes. Sox bounded through into their small clearing. He made straight for Marlee as he rushed right past Liam and found her at the campfire. He knocked her down and was licking her face while Park rushed over and hugged him saying, "Good boy, Sox. Good boy."

A few of the search party came through the break. A deputy radioed the rest of the team that the kids had been found. He had thermal blankets in his backpack, and he took one out for each of them. Collin brought a thermos full of hot chocolate and was pouring a mug for them each to share.

"The paramedic is nearly here," the deputy reported. "And Sheriff Cooper is on his way. He sent word back to your parents that you've been found safe."

This brought home to each of the kids, especially Marlee, what their little escapade had cost their parents in worry. Marlee was especially remorseful.

The deputy set off a flare so the others would know what direction to come.

When the paramedic arrived, he took out his gear to check everyone's temperature. Jem was nearing the hypothermic range. The paramedic took out a couple of more blankets and wrapped Jem up. "We'll need to get them back as soon as possible," he said to the deputy.

Everyone had fared pretty well, so they let Jem have most of the hot cocoa. The paramedic said they'd make better time if Jem were carried down, but he said no way, he was well enough to walk.

When the sheriff arrived, he approached the group to make sure they were all well. "Never go off like this without telling your parents. Leave a note if they are not home. It's a good thing Miss Pemberton remembered where you were going," he admonished them.

It started to snow, not a heavy fall, but enough that the kids knew just how lucky they were to be found. They might have spent the night in a snow storm.

"Wow! It's snowing! You might have just used up your Christmas wish, Marlee," Jem told her. "My mom will sure kill me now."

CHAPTER 17

The Stranger

The church had been set up as a command center. That's where the five of them found their parents waiting when they returned. Dr. Millman had been called and was awaiting their arrival. He checked Jem first and found that though he was pretty cold, he had not suffered hypothermia. None of them had to be treated medically. He recommended they all go home and warm up before going to sleep. "They all seem to be well, all things, considered," he told their parents.

"You can thank Liam and Park, they knew what to do. And Park luckily had a matchbook in the bottom of his backpack, and that saved our lives," Marlee told them.

Everyone realized this could have had a far worse outcome, so before they left, Marlee gave another praise prayer. She told the Lord she had been foolhardy but had learned her lesson and wouldn't do such a foolish thing again. If the parents hadn't been so relieved to have their children back safe and sound, they would have burst out laughing. Marlee certainly had a refreshing honesty when she prayed.

Miss Belle had come when she had heard they were missing and gave Marlee a hug. "Marlee, my love, you are destined for great things. You are a one of a kind if the Lord ever made one," Miss Belle told her.

"But, Mis Belle, everyone is a one of a kind," Marlee said.

"But you, Marlee, are at the top of the pile."

That night, Marlee told the Lord she was sorry once more. *I can't believe we didn't find more clues than that old log,* she mused. If it had been a real clue, it was likely that others would have deciphered it and located the treasure already. *I don't know why I thought I could just waltz up there and walk away with a fortune in gold. What did I think? That I would find the cabin and look down and say, "Oh what a lovely pile of gold is sticking out of the ground?" Miss Belle might think I'm destined for great things, but I think I'm a big goof. Oh well,* she concluded, *I can tell this to my grandkids. That is if Dad lets me live. He's not going to be any too pleased that I put Mom through this with her so soon out of the hospital.*

Thanksgiving was over, and it was beginning to look like Christmas in Christmas. Marlee's parents went easy on her since she was sorry and had learned her lesson. Jem's mom didn't kill him either, though he got a good dressing down. Mr. O'Brien didn't have the heart to scold his sons, as the sheriff said what Liam had done had saved their lives. The wall of pine boughs had been a great idea, though it was mistakenly attributed to Liam when it had been Marlee's idea.

Mr. Trumbull had come home, and Jem resumed going out to see him a couple of afternoons each week. They had to postpone the yard work until it got warmer in the spring. Jem said it didn't matter as there was no way he could come up with enough money to buy the stove in the amount of time left before Christmas. He planned to give his mom the money and tell her he would keep working for the rest.

Jem wondered why everyone thought Mr. Trumbull was rich. Maybe it was because he lived in the biggest house in town, a mansion compared to the rest of them. Jem was beginning to believe that all Mr. Trumbull had was his social security check. Mr. Trumbull no longer made his daily trip into town and was relying on Jem more and more. Jem noticed when he brought in the mail there were a lot of bills from his hospital stay. He wondered if Mr. Trumbull would be all right.

Marlee remembered to talk to the pastor. The benevolent committee had sent a Thanksgiving basket out to the Hamilton family. She knew they had included some much needed funds in the bottom of the basket. She spotted Hayden from time to time and admitted she looked discouraged, so she was pretty sure Mr. Hamilton had not yet found a job. She was certain Hayden would let her know as soon as he did. Marlee worried that she had done the wrong thing and given Hayden and her family a false sense of optimism.

Mrs. Madison had returned to health and was back to work at Belle's and Beaus. Patrick's father had fully recovered, except that they had not been able to buy another pickup truck. She wasn't sure what Mr. O'Brien was doing without a pickup as he needed it for his job.

Mrs. Hudson's students were finishing up their history projects, but Marlee was still struggling with hers, and that required frequent trips to the library. Patrick and Jem had finished their research, so she had the boxes of old papers to herself. Marlee had asked Miss Pemberton if she knew about an inscription at the cabin, but Miss Pemberton said she'd never heard of such a thing. That was after Miss Pemberton told Marlee that it was a good thing Marlee was still alive to ask her questions about old Jedediah Smith. Otherwise, there would be a sad story to have to record in the annals of Christmas's history.

Marlee noticed a stranger had come to town. He was staying at the Bed and Breakfast and took his meals at Miss Belle's. Marlee would see him walking around Christmas, taking in all the decorations and window displays. Most people in town didn't take much notice of him. Perhaps they thought he was an early tourist. Marlee was curious because he was dressed in a suit and tie every day, and most tourists did not dress up to come to town.

It was now time for the Nativity Night cast to be fitted for their costumes, and they all assembled on the second floor of the library. Much to Marlee's surprise, the stranger was there, and he was taking the time to look at all the exhibits. This would be a great day, Marlee thought because she would get to see the Baby Jesus figure for the first time. Miss Pemberton promised her she could stay behind when she opened its box.

Jem complained that his costume looked like a dress, and everybody laughed. Overall, the costumes fit pretty well, and Mrs. Stewart said since there were so few alterations to make, she would have them back in a week. She took all of them with her so she could have them dry-cleaned so they wouldn't smell musty.

Everybody left with Mrs. Stewart except Marlee who was staying behind so Miss Pemberton could show her the Baby Jesus figure. Miss Pemberton took her over to the closet where the box was kept. Marlee was surprised when Miss Pemberton turned to the stranger and told him she was ready.

She wasn't sure what this meant, but at this point, Marlee was more interested in looking at the figure. The stranger picked up the box and set it down on a table. Miss Pemberton took the key out of her pocket to open it up. She never let anyone know where she kept the key hidden in the library. It was all so mysterious. Marlee wasn't sure why they went to all this trouble for the Baby Jesus figure, even if it was old.

Miss Pemberton unlocked the box and lifted the lid. The stranger said, "Stunning." Marlee peered into the box, and her first impression was that it just looked like a painted wooden doll. She wasn't sure what she expected, perhaps a radiant glow, or a golden halo, or some kind of light to shine forth. Marlee was disappointed, as it looked faded, old, and uninspiring. How a legend could grow up around this figure, she could not imagine.

The stranger asked Miss Pemberton if he could remove it from the box to examine it more thoroughly, and she let him. He carefully held it up and then turned it over. He took a magnifying lens out of his pocket and looked through it at the paint, which Marlee couldn't understand because it was clearly faded and chipped in a couple of small places.

"This is very interesting. May I take photos?" Marlee didn't know who the stranger was, but he had clearly lost his mind.

Miss Pemberton agreed to that and Marlee wondered what on earth was going on. Was the town going to sell it or something? Who on earth would pay for an old wooden doll, even if it was the Baby Jesus? Besides, he apparently didn't respect the legend of the Christmas wish the way he was turning it over and over and once he even hung it upside down by its feet.

He took his photos and returned the figure to the box. "This is indeed special. You know the first nativity dates to the early 1200s. A couple of hundred years later, the idea had spread throughout Europe. I think this may be an early example, possibly from the Gothic era, and if it is, you could be looking at millions," he said.

Miss Pemberton stepped back, holding her hand to her heart as if she was going to faint and said, "Oh my, wait until I tell the mayor."

Marlee blurted out, "Are you talking dollars? Millions of dollars?"

"Why yes," the stranger said. "Of course, it is possible that it is later, Reformation perhaps. Early carvings such as this one were all coated in chalk and then painted. They are quite rare because during the religious contentions of the Reformation, so many of them were destroyed. It is possible this one survived, or it could be a later replacement for one that had been destroyed."

"Mister, who are you?" Marlee blurted out impolitely.

"Marlee, this is Mr. Addison. He is from Sotheby's in New York," Miss Pemberton said, realizing she hadn't introduced him in her excitement to show him the figure.

"I am a religious art appraiser. We ran across a reference to this figure in an art book recently. I called your mayor to see if I could come and examine it. If it's what I think it is, this will put your little town on the map. There are thousands of people who will travel from all over the world to see this. That is unless you want to sell it. It really should be specially housed in a case with the right environment for it, so that it does not deteriorate any further."

"And to think I picked this figure for my history project! Plus, I get to hold it on Nativity Night. Wait until everyone finds out it's a million-dollar baby!" Marlee said enthusiastically.

"Marlee, you mustn't tell anyone until I have a chance to talk to the mayor," Miss Pemberton said. "He might not want anyone to know just yet."

"Mr. Addison," Miss Pemberton said turning to him. "We are not prepared to secure this figure against those who become aware of its potential value. Our festival is coming soon, and we don't want to risk it being stolen. Would you please not release this information to the press? The mayor and council will determine what our next steps are, and the mayor won't want to proceed until the festival is over. Marlee, here, is our Mary this year. She will be holding the Baby Jesus figure shortly after midnight on Christmas morning. She is our 150th Mary to hold this very same figure, so you see it is special to us whether or not it is valuable. It is quite a night. I wish you could stay and see it."

"I have to tell you since it has been used for a 150 years it has held up well. I do think you should let us determine its age and style so we can give you a valuation, if for no other reason than to have it properly insured. And I wish I could stay for your Nativity Night, but I must return to New York. Take special care of this, Marlee, now that you know you are holding 'a million-dollar baby' as you put it," he said and smiled at her.

"So that I may tell the mayor, you mentioned its age as being from the I think you called it the Gothic period. If it's later than that, is it still valuable?" Miss Pemberton asked.

"Oh yes, maybe not quite as much, but there is no doubt this is quite the valuable item," Mr. Addison answered her.

Marlee decided she needed to research both the Gothic period and the Reformation for her project, so she'd have to see Miss Pemberton about finding an encyclopedia or some art books or whatever. Mr. Addison helped put the box back into the closet, and Miss Pemberton made sure she locked both it and the closet door behind her.

"Marlee, I must caution you not to say anything about this conversation. It is critical that no one finds out that this figure is valuable. We would not be able to secure it properly against anyone who wished to steal it. Please, say nothing."

"I promise, Miss Pemberton."

Marlee returned to her boxes of papers with renewed enthusiasm for her project. She worried her report would be boring though, since she would not be able to reveal the figure's value. Mr. Addison had mentioned a reference to this Baby Jesus in an art book. Perhaps he knew if that came from a newspaper account. She would ask Mr. Addison if he could tell her precisely what she should look for.

She spent the rest of the afternoon looking and finally found something of interest. She found an old newspaper article where Mr. Smith had been interviewed before his death. It was dated 1909, the year before he died. Oh, look at this! Smith's best friend was Hiram Trumbull. Maybe Mr. Trumbull had some information about his ancestor's friendship with Jedediah. She didn't think he could have the gold since he died before Mr. Smith. But perhaps there were clues left in the house. She'd have to ask Jem if he knew anything about it.

She picked up the newspaper to take it down to Miss Pemberton to be copied. She wanted to include Smith's picture in her paper and also to study his appearance. After all, she'd done what Miss Pemberton had and "touched the same things he touched." She made a note to ask Miss Pemberton if she might be allowed to touch Smith's Bible in the display case.

She handed the newspaper to Miss Pemberton and asked her to make a copy of the photo for her. Just as Miss Pemberton opened the lid of the copy machine, she said, "Marlee, did you see this?"

"What is it?" Marlee asked.

"Look above Jedediah's head!"

Marlee couldn't believe it. In the photo was a log mantelpiece, the same log she had discovered at the cabin, and she could clearly read the inscription. It read "MT621."

The Clue

When Jem got home, his mother asked how it went.

"I hate this Christmas festival stuff!"

"Jem, what on earth brought this up?"

"If it weren't for this Nativity stuff, I wouldn't have to be dressing up like a girl."

"Jem, you're being silly. You're a shepherd. That's what people wore back then."

"How am I going to be able to run after a sheep in a dress? I'll probably fall down flat. Besides, I'm tired of all this Christmas stuff. Here I am, trying to write a history project I wouldn't have to do if we didn't have a festival. I need time to help Mr. Trumbull."

"And you're doing one of the nicest things a boy your age has ever done, and I am so proud of you. It's wonderful what you have already done." Mrs. Jordan was happy to know that Jem had found a man in his life, even if he was ninety-two years old. Without a dad, Jem had missed out on a lot of "dad" things and both his grandfathers were too far away to participate in his life actively.

"Besides, the whole town is caught up in all this festival stuff, and you're always at Marlee's," he complained.

"Jem, you know that is only temporary. You know why we have to participate in the sale. It will only be a few more weeks, I promise," she told him.

"What are you going to do about getting a new stove?" Jem asked.

He was really disappointed that he hadn't been able to get the full amount he needed. He would give her what he had earned so far but wished he had been able to make enough money to hand her proof a stove was on its way on Christmas morning.

Marlee stood without moving a muscle. "Do you know what it means? It just says MT621. Is that a mountain around here?"

"I never heard that any of these mountains were numbered like that, but check with Patrick. Maybe he's run into something, perhaps a plat number or deed," Miss Pemberton replied.

Marlee was happy to have resolved the mystery of the carving, but she wasn't sure it brought her any closer. Mr. Trumbull might know. She'd ask Jem if she and Patrick could be included in one of his visits with the elderly man.

She returned to the box of papers and did indeed run across the newspaper account that must have been referenced in the art book. It didn't contain any more information than what she already knew, and actually what Mr. Addison said about it was more helpful. She also found an article on Christmas and how it became commercialized in the 1800s with the addition of trees, cards, Santa in a sleigh pulled by reindeer, and Santa coming down chimneys to deliver gifts. It said even Jewish people were starting to adopt Christmas traditions.

There used to be sales "wars" between Macy's and Gimbel's department stores in New York City, although only Macy's was still there. The movie, *Miracle on 34th Street,* made the stores legendary. *I guess that tradition still continues,* she thought to herself. Christmas displays were put up before Thanksgiving, and stores were open before everyone had digested their Thanksgiving dinners. She read how Dickens' story, *A Christmas Carol,* came to associate charitable appeals with Christmastime, though Marlee could only afford to put a few coins in the Salvation Army bell ringer's bucket.

So now Christmas had become more Santa than Savior, and that was sad. Jesus's birthday had been appropriated into an occasion for excessive gift giving and massive sales drives. *Except in our small-town,* Marlee thought to herself. *Thankfully, we still make His birth the focal point,* though she wondered if her town would be allowed to continue having a festival in the future.

Hayden was avoiding Marlee. One time, she actually saw Hudson scowl at her. *I guess that means their dad hasn't found a job yet*, Marlee thought. She hoped she didn't do something foolish and get their hopes up for nothing. It probably did sound silly. A five-dollar bill is no more a lucky charm than an old wooden Baby Jesus figure. God doesn't hand out jobs or Christmas wishes just because you want him to.

She stopped by Belle's and Beaus after school. Who better to talk to about it than Miss Belle?

When Marlee stepped through the door, she didn't display her usual excitement. Miss Belle noticed that she was sullen and downcast.

"What on earth is the matter, Marlee?" Miss Belle said as she came around the counter to give her a hug.

"How do you know something is wrong?" Marlee asked her.

"Because you didn't nearly take my door off coming in here," Miss Belle said with a smile. "I haven't seen you for ages. I'm sure glad you, your brother, and your friends didn't perish up on that mountain."

"Don't scold me, Miss Belle. I feel bad enough already. I'm sorry I didn't stay longer to talk to you at the church. We were so cold all we wanted was to get home."

"Come over here, and tell me what's got you down this time," Miss Belle said.

"I think I did something very foolish."

"We've all done something very foolish, Marlee," Miss Belle said.

"But this might have eternal consequences."

"Oh dear. That serious? You had better tell me the whole thing." Miss Belle took Marlee over to a booth so they could talk. Miss Belle sat so she could see if a customer came through the door.

"You know the Hamiltons, Hayden and her brother, Hudson?" Marlee asked her.

"I know of them, but I don't believe they've been in here before," Miss Belle responded.

"Well, you know they are not a family of means. They live in the trailer park. Mr. Hamilton lost his job two years ago. I think he worked in one of those factories in Henderson that closed."

"Yes, I heard about that. The church sent them a basket for Thanksgiving," Miss Belle said.

"That's the family. Well, Mr. Hamilton, the whole family really, are discouraged that he hasn't been able to find work. I saw Hayden in the girl's bathroom. I think she was crying about it. Anyway, you remember the five dollars you gave me last Christmas, and I said I was waiting for something special to spend it on?"

"Yes, I remember. You mean you still had it?"

Marlee nodded.

"All that time?"

Miss Belle couldn't believe a child wouldn't go right out and spend it, but that was Marlee for you.

"I gave it to Hayden," Marlee admitted.

"What's foolish about that?" Miss Belle asked.

"Wait, there's more," Marlee said.

"Go on," Miss Belle said. She was intrigued and couldn't wait to hear the rest of this story.

"At first, she wouldn't take it because she didn't want my pity. But I told her it wasn't my money, it belonged to Jesus, and he was giving it to her, so she had to take it."

"But that's good." Miss Belle said. She knew Marlee had a heart of gold, giving her friend what she knew Marlee probably needed herself.

"Wait, there's more."

What could be more? Belle wondered.

"I told her there was a string attached. I told her it was praise money and not pity money."

"I'm not sure I follow you," Miss Belle said.

"Well, pity money means you're asking God for something, but you're asking out of fear and worry. Praise money is when you're thankful, like for the job your father is going to get. And I prayed a praise prayer with her, right there in the bathroom, thanking God for that job."

"I still don't see how that is foolish," Miss Belle said, still wondering what Marlee had done that upset her so.

"The Hamilton family aren't believers. They don't go to church, and I not only thanked God for a job, but I also thanked God for giving him one that was better than the one he lost. And now Mr. Hamilton is still out of work, and I think they will never believe God or come to church, and it's all my fault," Marlee finished.

"Oh, Marlee, you are a wonder that you are. Not a thing you did was foolish. You stepped out in faith, my dear, and I have no doubt that you will see Mr. Hamilton get that job. That was quite a beautiful thing to do for that family, yes indeed. But you keep praying and praising God for that job, and before you know it, I think you'll see the answer."

"That's just it, Miss Belle. I failed. Once I asked Hayden to pray, I'm afraid I got distracted from it, and I haven't been praying or praising. What with my baby sister and my history project and getting caught up in being Mary, I have failed. I told God I was sorry for making a lucky charm out of a five-dollar bill and an old wood figure of Jesus."

"I don't think you think of them as lucky charms. There is nothing wrong when we exercise our faith. You gave that five dollars to Hayden in faith, and your 'Christmas wish' is nothing more than a prayer you are asking God to answer. That's how you should look at it, and it's not too late to resume praying and praising God for Mr. Hamilton's job. Abraham waited twenty-five years remember?"

"Mr. Hamilton can't wait twenty-five years!" Marlee said.

"I don't believe he'll have to. You wait and see. Didn't I tell you? You are destined for great things, Marlee. You exhibit great faith for a thirteen-year-old young lady. He'll answer that prayer when you are least expecting it. Don't you know God loves a good surprise!"

Marlee eventually caught up to Jem and Patrick after school and showed them the picture in the newspaper.

"I found this. Look at the inscription."

"MT621. What does it mean?" Patrick asked.

"Well, I hoped we could go out and see Mr. Trumbull. I found a newspaper article that said Hiram Trumbull was Jedediah's best friend."

"Yeah, that's his great grandfather. I could ask him if he knows what MT621 means, but I got to tell you, Mr. Trumbull is quite touchy if he thinks people are snooping around about the gold."

"Would he mind if we came with you one day?" Marlee asked him.

"What? Us go out there? Not me, leave me out of this. His house is haunted," Patrick said.

"No, it's not, Patrick. It's just run down. I've been in his house hundreds of times. Besides, I thought you didn't believe that kind of stuff. I'll ask him, Marlee, but if he says yes, don't you dare ask him anything about the gold."

"Why is that?" she asked.

"Because he's had to chase people off his property who want to go digging in his yard and ransacking his house, and he already knows the gold's not there. No one will believe him, and he is tired of the whole thing. Besides, he's not back to his regular self after coming down with pneumonia."

"That is terrible. I promise, but please don't forget to ask if we can come and see him," Marlee reminded him.

Jem came back a few days later and said Mr. Trumbull would let them come out to see him. Mr. Trumbull said the first Hiram Trumbull left a journal that he had read several times but didn't remember any mention of a mountain six-twenty-one. Mr. Trumbull said he'd look through the journal again before they came. As far as he knew, the only mountain associated with Smith was the one Smith lived on. But then, Mr. Trumbull had no idea where Smith found his gold, and that could have been on a different mountain.

They had to push Patrick halfway to Trumbull's. He tried turning around several times until Jem reminded him that he was the county's top science wiz, and he should know better than to believe in haunted houses.

"For crying out loud, Patrick! Don't you know there's no such thing as haunted houses?" Marlee said. "Only Jesus came back from the dead, and even he said he was flesh and blood, not a ghost. Besides, Jem's been inside loads of times. You think he'd go back in if he were scared?"

Patrick shrugged as this made sense to him but decided he would still reserve judgment until after he had gone inside.

After they met Mr. Trumbull, they could see why Jem liked him, even though his house was as close as they come to looking like it was haunted. Patrick told Jem that they could have filmed a *Goosebumps* movie there, and Jem said he had the same thought. Patrick conceded he had definitely been irrational, though, as the house was just old and rundown, and it was true that haunted houses only existed in books and movies.

Mr. Trumbull said he'd been through the journal, and there was no reference to MT621 anywhere. So that put an end to it in Marlee's mind. She had no other idea where to look. Patrick had gone through the plat number and deed ledgers, and there was nothing even close to it.

She concentrated on finishing her history project because they all had to be turned in by the end of the week. Tomorrow night, they had their Nativity Night meeting at the library to go over their final instructions.

At the meeting, everyone said they were ready for dress rehearsal. Marlee had already tried riding the donkey they would use. Jem had been practicing at Bascombe's farm, and Mr. Bascombe said he was ready. The three kings said it would be a piece of cake to ride horses from the back of the church the short distance they had to go to the Town Square.

Everyone knew who would give them their cues. Marlee and her brother would come from one end of town, and Jem would come from the other, all timed to make sure Marlee and Park arrived first. They all were ready for dress rehearsal scheduled for the ninth. The mayor would make sure the lights all worked and that the microphone was set up so that Gracie could read her part over the loudspeaker. They picked Mr. Caldwell to read the Christmas story from the book of Luke.

Jem's mom was putting her fruitcakes into tins when he arrived home. She had been baking every night and only had a week left before she was finished. She hoped the sale was so successful that she would have to replenish her supply frequently. Marlee's mom had all her items finished, and she was putting price tags on them.

The town tree had arrived as scheduled, and volunteers were getting the finishing touches on the lights and ornaments. They would be testing all the lights for the Grand Illumination before too long, as the mayor wanted them to all work when they lit the whole square after announcing the birth of the Baby Jesus.

Miss Pemberton would have the box that held the Baby Jesus figure brought over to the manger for dress rehearsal. She had been guarding the key with her life, even though no one but she, Marlee and the mayor knew the figure had suddenly taken on an astronomical value.

Everyone thought Ben Johnson was sure to be their best Santa ever, and both Santa's Workshop and the hay wagon were ready to go. They were still hanging lights and silver bells in the pine grove, but they would be done in a day or so.

Sheriff Cooper and his deputies had set up first aid stations around town. They had a plan for any disaster should one occur which they were all praying wouldn't.

The Boy Scouts volunteered to handle the parking again. They were busy painting white lines on the grass so they wouldn't forget to leave room for cars to get out once they were parked.

It was a wonderland of Christmas from lights to decorations, and goodies everywhere you went to the carols that were being played on radios throughout all the stores in town. Every shop owner, baker, crafter, and vendor were eager for the Festival to begin.

Marlee wasn't sure how she felt the morning of dress rehearsal day. She was excited that she would get to hold the Baby Jesus figure for the first time though she couldn't make her wish today because it wasn't officially Christmas. Maybe Marlee felt nervous because she knew the Baby Jesus figure was valuable, or perhaps it was because she thought she jinxed the Christmas wish by doubting in it. Though Marlee had already seen the Baby Jesus figure, she was still disappointed that it wasn't more spectacular to look at. In any event, she still had time to make up her mind what to wish for since it kept changing, and she hadn't settled on any one thing.

She and Park had no difficulty riding the donkey in from their side of town. Park complained about how long the trip was. Several minutes after they arrived at the manger, they saw Jem, muttering about his dress and herding two sheep from the opposite direction. The kings received their cue, and a couple of minutes later, they arrived and dismounted their horses, which they tied to a small corral that had been set up to keep the donkey and sheep from wandering away. Mr. Caldwell read the birth account from the book of Luke over the loudspeaker. At the end of this, all the lights in town, including the tree, went out so that it would be as dark as possible, though because they were practicing in daylight, they couldn't see the actual effect.

During this blackout, they heard the "cries" of newborn Baby Jesus. And then Gracie, in her angel costume, climbed on top of the manger and with just one spotlight shining on her, said her lines, "Hosanna in the highest. Glory to God. Peace on earth to all mankind. A Savior has been born."

This period gave Marlee time to go over to the box at the back of the manger to retrieve the Baby Jesus figure. Then she would return to her position in the front of the manger before Gracie finished her lines. As soon as Gracie finished, the whole Town Square would be lit up in the Grand Illumination. Every shop and house around the square had put up lights.

Marlee heard her cue that signified that the blackout period had begun, so she went over to the box. She heard Gracie say her lines. She stared into the box, frozen in place. Gracie had finished, and everyone was expecting her to return with the "newborn baby." The microphone was on top of the manger, so no one could hear her. All she could say was, "The box is empty."

CHAPTER 19

The Theft

At first, everyone thought Marlee was joking. When Miss Pemberton looked for the third or fourth time into the empty box, she felt sure someone was playing a joke. "When I unlocked the box, it was there," she said.

No one knew what to do. Everyone came up to take a good look in the box. It quickly spread around town that the Baby Jesus figure was missing. Pretty soon, some wild theories were circulating about what had happened to it. Everyone was sure that whoever took it did so because they thought it was valuable. They would probably try to sell it quickly. What good was it otherwise? Miss Pemberton nearly had a heart attack because they had no idea what it was really worth. The disaster she was afraid of happening had happened. She wondered if she had let the town know its value, would it have made a difference?

Sheriff Cooper was called, and he put that special yellow tape around the manger so that it looked like a crime scene right out of the cop shows on TV. Marlee was tired of standing around when it didn't seem like anyone was searching the area for it. She didn't think it could have gotten far. Marlee did not remember passing anyone leaving town in a hurry while she and Jem were making their way on the donkey. It had to have gone missing before all the cast arrived because Marlee was sure she would have noticed if someone had come up behind her to open the box. The box itself was out of sight behind some hay bales at the back of the manger. Both sides of the structure were open. Still, she didn't think someone could have managed to go unnoticed.

When the mayor arrived, he was frantic. "How could this happen? How could this happen?" he muttered several times as if by saying it more than once it would not have happened at all.

"What do we have so far, Jeff?" he finally asked Sheriff Cooper.

"We have secured the crime scene. I would like to get everyone down to the station to start questioning them. The first thing to do is put together a time line," the sheriff told him.

"Okay, let's get that going. I'll inform everyone to head on down there while you finish up what you need to do here," the mayor said.

"And, Sam, try not to let them talk to each other. I don't want them comparing stories," the sheriff added.

The mayor explained to the group that they were not to converse between themselves and were not to discuss what they saw to anyone but the sheriff and his deputies. They could, if they wanted to, go over in their minds, what they remembered seeing or hearing. "No detail is too small, and do not hold anything back because you might have one small piece of the puzzle and think nothing of it until it is put with someone else's piece," the mayor told them.

I sure hope we figure this thing out, he thought. Perhaps he should offer a reward, but then he thought about canceling the festival altogether. The town would be disappointed, but there was no use proceeding if they didn't have the main attraction.

The sheriff left his fingerprint technician to dust the box for prints. There were too many fingerprints and too many smudges because no one had polished the box in many years. They found no real evidence since too many people had left footprints all over the grass, and no one drove a car anywhere close to the square. Everyone was baffled.

Tim Johnson was questioned first. Yes, he had carried the box from the library to the manger, but no, he had not seen Miss Pemberton open it, and no, he did not know whether it was locked or unlocked when he set it down. Tim said he had too many things on his list to do since everyone wanted him for last minute fixes. He had immediately left the area to get this list of work done.

Miss Pemberton was next, and she was near to tears. She had unlocked the box shortly after it had arrived, and no, she had not stayed right by it the whole time as there was no one in the area but people she knew. Miss Pemberton tried to remember everyone who had been in the area. She watched them setting up the microphone and the ladder behind the manger that Gracie would climb. A man was testing the spotlight, and a couple of others were hanging loudspeakers, and she saw the mayor somewhere around, of course. She was trying to remember if that was before or after the box was opened. Miss Pemberton swore the figure was in the box when she unlocked it and offered to take a lie detector test if they didn't believe her.

Marlee said she didn't see how anyone could have gone to the box before she did, but she did confess that she wasn't really paying attention to where everyone was standing. Marlee couldn't swear that everyone was in their proper places because she remembered being distracted by the animals. "I guess it's possible that someone could have gotten there first, but then, where would they have hidden it?" she told them.

Marlee suggested that the sheriff needed to find out if anyone had been seen leaving the back of the manger carrying a bag or blanket or something.

The rest of the cast were questioned, but they couldn't add any more than Marlee had. Eventually, the sheriff let them go. Mr. Bascombe had already taken his sheep back to his farm, and the donkey and horses were returned to their owners. All the kids went straight home because they hadn't expected to be this long, and they were all getting hungry.

Marlee sat silently at the table that night. Park couldn't stop talking about it, and their mother had lots of questions for him.

"Marlee, don't you have something to say about this?" her mother asked her.

"Yes, I do. First, whoever did this has cheated me out of my Christmas wish. And second, I intend to find out who it is in time for us to still have Nativity Night."

The following day, the mayor said there was a reward for the person who found the Baby Jesus figure. The time line had been published. Anyone who wanted a copy could stop by the station and pick one up from Sheriff Cooper. Two days passed, and they were no closer to solving the crime.

Marlee went over and over it in her mind. First, what was the motive to steal it? Well, she and Park had one, because Dad had the medical bills to pay. Liam and Patrick had a motive because their dad needed a pickup truck. Then there was Jem and his mother's stove and Hudson because his father was out of work. Gracie was too little, and besides she was on top of the manger. And then, of course, there was Miss Pemberton because she knew it was worth a lot of money.

She tried to figure out who had the opportunity to take it. That was much harder. Miss Pemberton had more chances to steal it, so she was the most likely suspect. She was the custodian of the box. She might have left the Baby Jesus figure back at the library and not even had it in the box when Tim Johnson carried it to the manger. But why would an eighty-two-year-old lady who took care of the figure all these years steal it now? She didn't think Miss Pemberton would be tempted to do so now that she knew it was worth perhaps millions. She wouldn't live long enough to spend that kind of money, and she didn't have anyone to leave it to.

Marlee didn't think Tim Johnson had much opportunity unless he lingered longer than he said he did, and Miss Pemberton was not paying attention. She said she unlocked the box after he left. Could she be mistaken? Had she done it before he left the area? The first person on his list of tasks swore he came back empty-handed, but he could have stopped anywhere and hidden the figure if he had been carrying it in a large bag of tools.

She was going to talk to Liam, Patrick, and Jem tomorrow just to make sure they didn't forget something important. Maybe if she asked them some questions, it would jog their memories. She'd get them all together, the five of them, to hash it out as soon as possible. She didn't want to waste any time trying to solve this mystery. She hoped Nativity Night would not be canceled. She wanted her Christmas wish.

She was also going to talk to the sheriff about making sure no one from town was missing or acting funny. After all, if someone left Christmas with the Baby Jesus figure determined to sell it, they would either be missing from town or acting guilty. She really couldn't imagine anyone in town being so brazen as to steal that figure. She asked the sheriff if all the pawnshops in the area had been contacted. He said yes, they even had a statewide network to identify stolen property of value and he had faxed the state police in Henderson so they could be involved. She was out of ideas.

When the five of them got together, she asked a lot of questions. Most of them couldn't answer a single one. Marlee then asked them to make a list of everyone they remembered seeing in the area, whether it was someone passing by or one of the people involved in the dress rehearsal. "Don't even leave your own name off the list. I mean you must put everyone on the list that you remember seeing," she told them.

She went by the library and asked Miss Pemberton if she would mind doing the same thing. At this point, Miss Pemberton was so upset she said she was willing to do anything and that nothing was too big or too small if it led to the recovery of their figure. She said she didn't give a fig what it was worth, and Mr. Addison could just keep his appraisal. She just couldn't stand to see something they had had for a 150 years lost forever. Miss Pemberton almost burst into tears, but Marlee said not to worry. She was going to solve this thing if it was the last thing she did.

The next day, she retrieved everyone's lists, but after studying them, she still had no clues. Marlee took off for Miss Belle's. She didn't know if Miss Belle had been out on the square while the dress rehearsal was going on.

"I did stop by for a bit. I had to come back here before you and Jem, and the three kings arrived though, so I wasn't there when you said the box was empty."

"Did you see anybody that looked out of place, Miss Belle?"

"No. I saw the fellows working on the loudspeakers and the spotlight. The mayor, but only because he came by to get a box of lights left over when mine were put up. He said he was busy all day, getting the lights up at Town Hall and couldn't stop to chat. Everyone seemed in a hurry that day. I'm sorry I can't be of more help," Miss Belle said.

Marlee went to see Mr. Caldwell who could add no clues. Then she went to see Pastor Mac and Dr. Millman, but neither of them had been able to get to the square to see any part of the rehearsal.

She had pretty much ruled out everyone in the cast even though each one had a motive. She just couldn't see where they had the opportunity.

She went by Town Hall to see if Mayor Donnelly was there. It was when she entered the doorway that she had the answer. She met the mayor in his office.

"Marlee, what can I do for you?" he greeted her.

"Why did you do it?" she asked him straight out.

"What? What are you talking about?" the mayor said.

"Why did you take the Baby Jesus figure, Mayor?"

"Well now. You tell me why you suspect me? Me, of all people?"

"I've been over all the possibilities. I don't believe any of my castmates had the opportunity though they all had a motive. Every one of us has an unexpected need for money this Christmas. But I am pretty sure I would have seen someone go behind me to take the baby out of the box, and then where would they have hidden it? I checked the stack of hay, thinking maybe they had hollowed out a spot and put it in there, but I looked, and nothing was amiss. I had everyone make a list of the names of the people they remember seeing. Only Miss Pemberton was at the manger for any length of time, but she said she'd gotten tired of standing there, so she went out and sat on one of the benches.

"The guys that were hanging the loudspeakers and the spotlight had a bird's eye view and said they remembered seeing you on the green earlier in the day. But I remember when the theft took place, you weren't there. I thought it was odd that you wouldn't come to see the Grand Illumination since you were so adamant about making sure all the lights were working. Then I talked to Miss Belle, and she said you weren't there because you were busy hanging the lights here at Town Hall. Only when I came in, I saw there were no lights up. Miss Belle said you were at her store with a box, which she said was an extra box of lights left over from when you hung her lights up. That's what you told her, and she would have no reason not to believe you. Inside that box was the Baby Jesus figure, wasn't it? I just want to know why you did it," Marlee finished.

She was mad and started again. "Is it because you know how much it's worth and you think you're protecting it? You think that we would settle for some substitute on Nativity Night? The crowd wouldn't care. But I'm Mary this year, and I won't be cheated out of getting to hold that figure."

"No, Marlee, it's not that. But I have to hand it to you. I wasn't sure anyone would figure it out, and before you get angry with me again, I was going to return it for Nativity Night. I am going to address the town tomorrow night. It's the night before the festival begins. Make sure you're there. You'll understand it all, I promise you. And, Marlee, please don't let anyone know. I want to be the one to tell them. I really need to address this town tomorrow night. I have something important to say."

"All right, but poor Miss Pemberton is over there at the library, and I think she's crying her eyes out. She at least deserves an explanation from you."

"Oh, Marlee. Do you think I could risk Miss Pemberton having a heart attack? Especially since Mr. Addison let us know it's quite a bit more valuable than we realized. She's known from the beginning. Ah, now I see I've got one on you. Yes, she's quite the actress that one. Even I am impressed with how well she did."

"That better be some message is all I have to say. I'll try not to be as mad as I am right now at both of you."

"Marlee, I don't think you have a clue what a wonder you are. Belle tells me you are destined for great things, and I agree. She has a lot of pride in the young lady you're growing up to be and your best friend, Jem. Not many kids his age would take it upon themselves to keep an elderly man company as he has. I'm not sure how much you've influenced him. His mother says she gives you a lot of the credit. I really am sorry I had to do this to you, but I think you'll see

my reasoning is sound. Just get everybody over to the square tomorrow night."

Marlee was tired. She had struggled with her Christmas wish
and gotten everybody lost and almost dead up on Smith Mountain.
She had lost a baby sister and felt cheated that, not only had she not
been able to see her, but she also would never get to know her. She
had spent way too much time on her history project and was not sure
she had even done it well. She had given Hayden something to hope
for that she wasn't sure would happen. She wished she could go back
to being twelve when life seemed easier.

Then she remembered Mr. Spafford, faith, and "it is well with
my soul." She remembered her sister, Faith, and knew no matter
what she would trust God. Sure, she made mistakes as everyone did.
But that would not stop her, and if Miss Belle thought she was destined for great things, so be it. From this point on, she vowed to be
the best Marlee Madison in the world. And if there were any truth
to the Christmas wish legend, she would come up with the best wish
yet, one that she promised would honor the Lord above all else.

CHAPTER 20

The Mayor's Speech

"**L**adies and Gentlemen, and young people, I have asked you all to be here tonight as I have something to say that has been weighing on my heart for some time. Let me start by saying that our Baby Jesus figure has been found."

At this, the whole town rang out in applause, cries, whistles, and any other sound they could make to show their joy at having the figure returned.

"I want you to know that I am the culprit, I took Jesus out of Christmas."

Now the applause turned into boos and jeers.

"It was young Marlee Madison here who figured it out, and let me tell you, she was madder at me than you are now. I told her I would explain why I did it so, please listen.

"For 149 years, the center of this town has been the celebration of Christmas. Everything we stand for culminates on December 25. I believe that in all those years, this town has honored and glorified the little baby whose birth we celebrate. And most everyone in this town doesn't just celebrate Christmas, we celebrate Easter, too.

"But we all have seen that over the years, decades really, the world is chipping away at the real celebration of Christmas. We have traded the manger for malls, the Savior for Santa, candy canes for crèches, and gifts galore instead of grace. Without the Christ in Christmas, you get mas, and it sounds like what it is, a mess.

"I am proud of this town because we come together when we are in need. I am proud of this town because year after year we put on a Christmas festival that reminds the many visitors who come to participate that Christmas is about Christ. But I am afraid. I am worried that we will be surrounded by bigger towns with extended shopping hours, sale prices we cannot compete with, and that as new generations grow into adulthood, more and more people will lose the traditions that make Christmas meaningful.

"Think of it this way, what other holiday causes us to eat too much, spend too much, and take our gifts back to the stores the next day to get something we really wanted? What other holiday causes us to run from mall to mall, stand in line for hours, shop in stores that are open all night long, or worse that are open on Thanksgiving, a day we should be spending in thankfulness to God for our blessings, not out at the malls accumulating more stuff. How many people spend more time waiting in line to pay than enjoying time with their families? It's nuts. Who knew Christmas would be measured by successful Black Fridays and Cyber Mondays?

"Christmas should be about family, friends, community, and Jesus. I am guilty of reducing Christmas to the crass, the commercial, and the competition. I talked to Miss Pemberton about what we could do to increase attendance. The more people who attend, the more dollars we make. I have concluded that that approach does not give honor and glory to the Baby.

"The world tells us we need more trees and bells, lights and candy, gifts and parties, cards and fruitcakes, big meals, and now even big blow up things for the front yard. But I tell you all we need is to remember that without Christ, all you have is mas. We need to spend more time telling everyone why that little Baby Jesus figure is in that manger. That's just the beginning of his story. We need to be telling the rest of it. Oh, I know, I worry that the day may come when we're told we have to stop presenting our Christmas festival and holding Nativity Night. I would like to think that that day will never come, but I imagine it will. Now there is one more thing to be said. There will be some news that I cannot release until after Christmas."

Again, there were boos.

"I'm sorry, but I don't want to take away from the festival. I want everyone to have a great time from now until Christmas. There will be time after things have settled down. Marlee, come up here, please."

What on earth does the mayor want with me? Marlee thought.

"I posted a reward for the return of our Baby Jesus figure, so this rightfully belongs to you." He handed her a check for five hundred dollars, but she had no idea what she would do with it. "I don't want it, Mayor. I didn't really find it," she whispered to him.

"Well, it's made out in your name, so you figure it out later," he whispered back.

"Thank you, Mayor," she said as the town applauded. As a matter of fact, it was a standing ovation.

Her mother looked at Park who just shrugged his shoulders. Neither had any idea Marlee had solved the so-called crime. *Funny way for the mayor to make a point, but it did get our attention,* Jenna Lee mused. Her daughter, *did I really give birth to that child, or did she come from some magical place?*

Everyone broke up and went home to get ready for tomorrow's festivities. The crowds would start coming, and it meant a lot of extra work, but everyone enjoyed it as a way to make Christmas special for themselves, and they hoped, for their visitors.

CHAPTER 21

The Festival
Goes On

By all accounts, it was one of their best festivals in recent years. Miss Belle's pies were a big hit, and she couldn't make enough of them. Elsa Jordan heard time and time again that she needed to open a bakery so they could buy her treats all year long. Marlee's mom sold every one of her crocheted items. The hidden ornaments, which weren't that hard to find, were a big hit, and some visitors met on the square to trade coupons with each other. The sheriff had only a couple of people come into the first aid stations, and most of them were kids, horsing around, who skinned a knee or an elbow. They had their largest crowd ever who gathered on opening night for the Christmas tree lighting and who stayed to sing Christmas carols on the square.

They were making continuous runs of the "one horse open sleigh" through the grove of trees to Santa's Workshop. Ben Johnson was so good at being Santa that even the grownups believed in him. Everybody went home tired each night but ready to do it again the next day.

Jem still spent a lot of time out at Mr. Trumbull's. He said he hoped Mr. Trumbull would be well enough to come to see him shepherd his sheep on Nativity Night. Marlee still couldn't decide what her Christmas wish would be, but since she knew the town might benefit in some way from having so valuable a Baby Jesus figure, she wasn't stressing over it anymore. She told her mom and dad she was worried more over what she should do with the reward money. Marlee knew her parents needed it, but so did the Hamiltons and so did the O'Briens and so did Jem. They told her she didn't need to do anything with it for the time being, but she still felt guilty. She didn't actually find the Baby Jesus figure, she just discovered who had waylaid it.

It would be time for Nativity Night soon. Marlee's parents went out to the library to see what Mrs. Hudson's class had done for the project and thought Marlee had an excellent write up on Mr. Smith and his acquisition of the Baby Jesus figure. She included lots of fascinating accounts of the legend of the Christmas wish.

Before she knew it, Marlee had her Mary costume on, and her father was driving her and Park out to where the donkey was waiting for them. Jem was out at Bascombe's farm, and Mr. Bascombe was giving him some last minute tips. Mr. Trumbull was waiting in his front parlor and had decided to follow Jem into town, at a safe distance, so Jem wouldn't see him and get nervous. It would be his first walk into town since he returned from the center, but he thought he had enough stamina to make it all the way. Liam, Patrick, and Hudson were ready to make their royal visit. The box was sitting behind the hay, and Miss Pemberton looked inside several times to assure herself it was still there. She decided she was not letting it out of her sight this time. Miss Pemberton found a spot off to the side where she could sit, looking directly into the manger and at the box.

The crowd had lined up to follow Mary and Joseph as they made their way into Bethlehem on that wonderful night of Jesus's birth. They all arrived in the proper order. Jem never knew that Mr. Trumbull was following him. He had his hands full with the sheep and his "dress," which got tangled around his legs more than once. When everyone was assembled at the manger, Mr. Caldwell read the Christmas story from Luke. Then all the lights went out. There were a few who cried a little when they heard the cries of the newborn baby. Gracie climbed to the top of the manger and looked beautiful as she said her lines in the spotlight. There was no doubt Elsa was wiping her eyes with a Kleenex.

Marlee took her cue and found the Baby Jesus figure in the box as expected. Marlee felt awestruck to be holding it, and a Christmas wish popped into her head that she had not expected. *How odd*, she thought. Marlee stared down at the baby Jesus and thought, *I'm touching what he touched and what 149 other Marys have also held over the years.* She wondered what the real Mary thought when she first held her baby who was Emmanuel, God with us. Just as these thoughts passed through her mind, every light in town went on, and the Grand Illumination must have been seen clear to Henderson. She couldn't believe the cheers. They went on and on and on. *This is what it will be like when we have the second Advent of the Lord*, Marlee thought. The cheering, the lights, the music, and Jesus standing before us in the flesh.

Marlee was sad it was over. This year saw a lot of change in her, in her friends, especially Jem, and she was a little afraid of what the New Year might hold. She thought she heard someone whisper the name, Faith. Yes, *Faith*, and faith would always be a part of her life.

"Marlee, oh, Marlee!"

Marlee turned from putting the figure back in the box when she saw Hayden running up to her. "Oh, Marlee. I wanted to wait until the end to tell you."

It was just then that Marlee remembered it was after midnight, so this was Christmas Day.

"Merry Christmas, Hayden."

"Oh, Marlee, your prayer. My dad got a job. He's going back to his old factory. They are going to reopen." Hayden was beaming.

"Oh, Hayden, I am so happy for you! That's the best Christmas gift I could ever get," Marlee said, not knowing whether she should be relieved or grateful or both.

Hudson joined them and said, "I wanted to tell you, but Hayden said no. She had to be the one to tell you."

"I thought you looked like you were hiding something," Marlee said to him.

"You know the part of the prayer that thanked God for giving him a better job than the one he lost?" Hayden asked her.

"Yes," Marlee said, wishing she had prayed harder for Mr. Hamilton.

"They're making him foreman, at way more money that he used to make."

Marlee was stunned. God is good. "Oh, praise God, praise God," she said in just the way Miss Belle would say it.

"And, Marlee, Mom says this is the time for us to be making a new start. A new year and a new beginning. She wants us all to start coming to church."

Oh, Miss Belle, Marlee thought. *You are so right about our Lord. In his own time and when you least expect it.*

Marlee looked down at the plaque, and suddenly she knew.

"Everybody. Everybody, stop! Hudson, get the microphone."

He reached up top and pulled it down and handed it to her.

"Everybody, stop! Listen! Get the mayor, get the mayor," she said frantically.

She could clearly be heard on the microphone. People came running back, thinking something was wrong. The mayor made his way through the crowd.

"Marlee, what on earth?" the mayor asked her.

She put the mike down. "Oh my goodness." She thought she was going to faint. "I know where the gold is. I know where Jedediah hid the gold."

"What on earth are you talking about? Slow down, Marlee. Start from the beginning."

Clearly, the mayor was shocked and wasn't quite sure he caught everything she said.

By now, Jem, Patrick, Liam, Park, Hudson, Hayden, and even Mr. Trumbull, who had his arm around Jem's shoulder, were gathered around her. She looked at the crowd. Though it was thinning, some had stayed behind, curious about her sudden outburst.

"Okay, Mayor. You know that we went up the mountain looking for clues. Well, all I found was an old log that looked different from the others. We all thought it had something carved on it, but we couldn't figure what it was. Until one day, I was working on my history project, and I found a newspaper article from someone who actually spoke to Jedediah Smith right there in his cabin. I didn't see it, Miss Pemberton did. It was clear as a bell above his head. There was the log over his fireplace like a mantle, and the marking on it was MT621. Miss Pemberton said she didn't know what it meant, and Mr. Trumbull…"

Just then she looked at Mr. Trumbull who raised his head with a surprised look on his face, wondering how he could have anything to do with this story.

"Mr. Trumbull had an old journal from his great grandfather who was Jedediah's best friend. Surely, he would know what it meant. But there was nothing there, so I gave up. Patrick even checked all the plat books at the library and still nothing."

"I don't get it, Marlee. What are you saying?" Park said, still trying to figure out what a plat book was, and Marlee had him thoroughly lost.

"It's simple really. MT621 isn't a mountain."

"What is it then? You had me looking all over the place for mountains numbered 621," Patrick said, and he sounded irked that Marlee had sent him on a wild goose chase.

"It's so simple. I don't know why I didn't see it straight away."

"Marlee, you need to tell me where this is going because you have totally lost me." By now, the mayor was shaking his head, but then again, Marlee had figured out the mystery of who took the Baby Jesus figure. She was a smart one that she was.

"I'm sorry, Mayor Donnelly. MT is the book of Matthew."

"What does the book of Matthew have to do with the gold?" Jem asked.

"Matthew 6:21. It says where your treasure is, that's where your heart is. Or if you want to simplify, your treasure and your heart are in the same place," Liam stated, catching on to where Marlee was headed.

"Exactly, Liam. What's really funny is that ever since Mrs. Hudson told me that I would be Mary this year, I've been thinking and thinking and thinking what my wish was going to be. I even researched the legend as part of my history project. And then when the time came, this other wish popped right into my head, and I don't even know where it came from because it wasn't one that I had ever thought about."

"What wish was that, Marlee?" Hayden remembered back to last year when she was Mary, and she had known what her wish was going to be the moment she was told she would be Mary.

"It came from Jedediah's will, and it was 'lead us to it in your own time.' Read the plaque, Mayor."

"The heart of Christmas is the Christ Child."

"The gold is beneath this plaque," Marlee said simply.

That night, the whole town and many of the festival visitors stayed to watch the digging operation. Mrs. Jordan took Mr. Trumbull home as he said he was too tired to watch but to send Jem out after Christmas with a full account.

Mr. Johnson, Mr. Caldwell, and Mr. O'Brien dug for what seemed like hours, and the hole just kept getting wider and deeper. Marlee was beginning to think she could be mistaken, but no, she was sure she was right because of that wish that popped into her head unexpectedly. The crowd, however, started to mumble, and a lot of the visitors said it was time to go home. They didn't think they'd miss much if they left.

It was somewhere past two in the morning when Tim Johnson cried out, "We hit something!"

It took another hour for all the strongboxes to be removed from the hole, and they figured there was something around two hundred pounds of gold altogether.

"How did you figure it out?" Park asked her.

"I didn't. I can't explain it. It started when I picked up the Baby Jesus figure from the box. I really didn't understand that wish that popped into my head. And then I looked down at the plaque, and I suddenly realized that MT621 meant Matthew 6:21. And it just all came together in an instant. Honestly. It just happened. I can't explain it. Jedediah's will said God would lead us to it in his time."

"Not us, Marlee, you."

Miss Belle ran up to her and gave her the biggest hug, tears streaming down her face.

"Miss Belle, whatever on earth is the matter?" Marlee asked her.

"Oh, Marlee, did I not tell you that you were destined for great things? Oh, if only my Franks could see this. This is only the start, Marlee, this is only the start. God is not finished with you yet."

CHAPTER 22

A Sad Goodbye

Word quickly spread that Jedediah's gold had been discovered. Many sad treasure hunters couldn't believe how many times they had walked over that plaque. It turned out the gold amounted to over four million dollars. That was a strange year to celebrate Christmas because even the most devout had trouble keeping their minds off the odd events of the overnight hours.

In the following days, the town agreed that this should be the last of the Christmas festivals, and the mayor announced the secret he'd been keeping from them that the gold wasn't their only source of wealth. He was making plans to have the Baby Jesus figure taken to New York for Sotheby's to determine its age and value.

The town was divided over whether they should sell it to a prominent museum or open a bigger one in Christmas. It was Marlee who convinced them that they needed to tell the story of Jesus if they weren't going to have a festival anymore. She remembered that Mr. Addison said art lovers from all over the world would come to their little town to see the Baby Jesus figure. She wanted the town to explain the story of Christmas and the history of Christmas in the same museum. "It is what Jedediah would have wanted us to do," she told them, and they said she had a point.

The state took control of the gold, to begin with, but since it belonged to Jedediah fair and square, Miss Pemberton produced Jedediah's will, which said clear as a bell that he left his gold to the town. Of course, that didn't keep them from taking their share in taxes.

After there was an accounting by a CPA firm, the town received a handsome check. They would use it for the museum and also build a climate-controlled display case for their precious figure. They divided the remainder, and each family got an equal amount.

Marlee became a celebrity for a couple of weeks and was flown to New York City, all expenses paid, to appear on all the national news shows. She liked being on Fox and Friends the best. Ainsley Earhardt, one of the hosts, put her at ease, and because they were both believers, they had a lively conversation after they went off the air. Everyone told her she was a natural on TV, but she couldn't decide whether she wanted to be a TV journalist or a writer when her mother said it was actually okay to be both.

The governor couldn't be more elated that Christmas was now the most famous destination in the whole state. He agreed that if they were going to have visitors from all over the world, they would need to have Internet service, so the legislature passed a special appropriation for it. They would also require more hotels, so permits were issued to the big hotel chains to build just outside of town.

Patrick was already awarded a full scholarship to Virginia Tech after he won a third science fair. He told them he was not yet fourteen, but that didn't matter to them, they would be waiting for him once he graduated from high school.

In June, Mr. Trumbull took ill, and Jem was told he would not survive this time. In the end, Jem, and all the people who had grown to love Mr. Trumbull, gathered around his hospital bed to say goodbye, but it was Jem who held the old man's hand and sat by his bed, refusing to leave him for even a minute.

After the burial, they went back to the church for a repast when a man came up to Jem and handed him a letter. Marlee was there but vowed not to let her curiosity get the better of her. She knew that Jem really loved Mr. Trumbull, and he was deeply grieved at his passing, so she left him to have time to himself. She gave him a hug and told him she was there for him if he needed anything, and she left the church.

Jem didn't open the letter until he was home alone in his room.

It read:

My dearest Jeremy,

If you are reading this letter, then you know I have gone on to my heavenly home. Do not be sad, for I am now reunited with my beloved wife and son. Yes, I had a son, and if you look carefully in the cemetery, you will see that he and my wife were buried in the same grave.

My son was named Jeremiah, and he died at the age of thirteen. When he died, my wife and I shut ourselves away. We closed those red velvet curtains you never liked, and they never got opened again. I think I closed the curtains on my heart also, as there were no bright spots to be found in our lives after that. Once my wife died, I decided my life was over, too. And then you nearly ran me down. I never told you, but I wished you had killed me that day, but then I realized that would have been a terrible burden for you to bear, and I was sorry I thought it.

When you returned to rake my leaves, I started wondering what God was trying to say to me. When you told me your name was Jeremy and that you were thirteen, the icicles on my heart melted away.

I know God brought you into my life for a special reason. You are a young man of rare integrity and incomparable character. Not one soul in Christmas in all those years cared enough to make sure an old man was okay. When you came to visit me out at the center, I knew even before then that I could not love you more were you my own. I got the rare gift your father threw away, and I hope someday he will realize his mistake and try to repair what he has torn so badly.

I instructed my lawyer to give you this letter at my funeral. You will hear soon enough that I have left you my house and all its contents. There is also a small sum of money, which I would like your mother to set aside for your education. You have my permission to remove those old heavy red curtains if you like. Actually, since everything will be yours, you may do with it as you will.

I don't want you to be sad for long. Live a long, healthy, and happy life. If God lets me look down on you, know that I will. I wish you all the best that life has to offer, and I hope that my contribution will help your mother and you to make a wonderful life for yourselves and little Gracie.

Jeremy, thank you for opening the eyes and heart of an old man. You brought great joy to me in my last days upon this earth. If you think of me from time to time over the rest of your life, know this: God is good. I didn't understand why I lost my son, but he gave me a great treasure when he brought you into my life.

With All My Love and Respect,
Hiram Jeremiah Trumbull

Jem folded the letter. He was profoundly grieved that Mr. Trumbull died, and he knew he wouldn't be able to go out to his house for some time.

He told his mom what Mr. Trumbull wrote in the letter. Jem spoke so softly she almost couldn't hear him. "I'm sorry we can't live in the house for a while. But we'll be able to sell this one, and I know that will be a big help to you, maybe even enough to start your bakeshop, but I just can't do it yet, Mom, I'm sorry." Jem started to cry again.

"Oh, Jem, I know it's too soon. I don't want you to worry about me. It will take time for his death to settle in, and you'll miss him for a long time. It's okay to cry. He was a wonderful man, and what you did for him makes me so proud. Someday, you'll find yourself thinking about him, and it will bring a smile instead of tears. I promise. You'll be able to remember all the happy times you had, and it won't tug at your heart so."

"Thanks, Mom."

School was out for the summer, and right now, he didn't know what he would do with himself except try to remember everything he didn't want to forget about Mr. Trumbull.

What a year this has been, he thought. *Marlee, finding Smith's gold, me, bumping into Mr. Trumbull. Those turned out to be the best days of our lives.*

Jem knew Christmas would never be the same, now that they had a million-dollar Baby Jesus figure that would be displayed in a million-dollar museum. Plus, each family got some of the money from the gold.

Life is funny, Jem thought. Here he was worried about getting his mother a stove for Christmas, and now he owned the biggest house in town. Well, he hoped somehow his mother could open a bakery because she really did make the best baked goods in the state.

Jem wondered what changes lay ahead. His life had undoubtedly changed forever. So had Marlee's. And Patrick? It looked like his future was lining up.

He knew he needed to adjust to these changes, but he would go slowly. He had the summer before him. The Trumbull house wasn't going anywhere. When he felt better, he would take his friends out there. They had been in the house before, but now they would explore it at their leisure. Maybe Marlee would unlock more mysteries. No one knew where Jedediah found his gold in the first place. Who knew what she might uncover? Marlee sure had a knack for solving mysteries.

His mind drifted off as he wondered what it was like in heaven. *I'll see him again*, Jem said to himself, and the thought comforted him. His eyes closed, and a very tired young man took a very much needed nap.

Acknowledgments

My sincerest thanks to Joy Brunnelson for your invaluable help, to Margaret Green for your love and support, to Charles Brunnelson for your encouragement every step of the way, to Ben Brunnelson for your phenomenal talent, and to Bill Green for your helpful suggestions.

About the Author

M s. Brunnelson lives in Germantown, Maryland, and is retired from the US Department of Commerce. She is a mother of two and grandmother of six. She has been studying the Bible since becoming a Christian at the age of fifteen and graduated from California Baptist University (when it was still a college) in the early 1970s. She and her husband attend Cornerstone Chapel in Leesburg, Virginia. She received her first Agatha Christie novel as a young teenager from her grandmother and has been an avid fan of mysteries ever since. Besides taking care of her family, she has one goal in life, to share the good news of Jesus Christ. In this first book, she hopes you will find the perfect blend of both her passions: the good news of Jesus and a good mystery story!

CPSIA information can be obtained
at www.ICGtesting.com
Printed in the USA
FSHW021341191019
63182FS